FIRST $13

Briefly Told
Lives

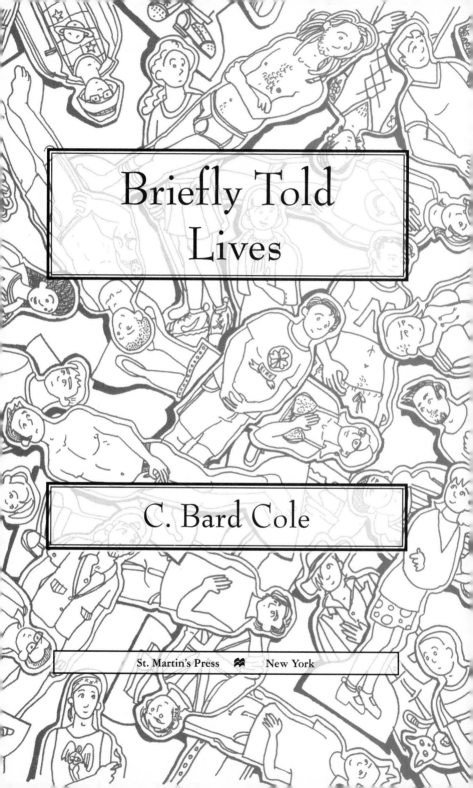

Briefly Told Lives

C. Bard Cole

St. Martin's Press ⚓ New York

"On a Railroad Bridge, Throwing Stones" appeared in *Christopher Street* #227 (July 1995).

"Used to Dream" appeared in *The Mammoth Book of Gay Erotica* (1997). Some portions appeared in the chapbook *Tattooed Love Boys* (1994).

"Selected Lives in Brief" appeared in *Riotboy* #3 (1997).

"A Case Study" appeared in *Dirty,* volume II, no. 2 (1995), and in the anthology *Flesh & the Word IV: Gay Erotic Confessionals* (1997).

"Additional Selected Lives In Brief" appeared in *Holy Titclamps* #16 (1998).

An earlier version of "Young Hemingways" appeared in the chapbook *Young Hemingways* (1995).

"Anniversary" appeared in *Blithe House Quarterly* #1 (1997) and in *Men on Men* 7 (1998).

"That's How Straight Boys Dance" appeared in *Blithe House Quarterly* #5 (1998).

www.stmartins.com

ISBN 0-312-25351-6

First Edition: August 2000

10   9   8   7   6   5   4   3   2   1

For Joey, Laurence, and Aldo

Acknowledgments

For their assistance and support, I am always grateful to Aldo Alvarez, Glenn Belverio, David Bergman, Perry Brass, Dick Gallablatt, Robert Kirby, Chris Leslie, Michael Lowenthal, Joey Manley, Joan K. Peters, Laurence Roberts, Bob Satuloff, Sarah Schulman, D. Travers Scott, Tom Steele, Sara Valentine, Katharine Weber, and my mother and sisters. I also want to thank Tony Arena, Aaron Jason, Travis Jeppesen, Matty Pritchard, Chris Schneider, Ned Schenck, and Brian Sloan for their inspiration and friendship.

Contents

Briefly Told
Lives

On a Railroad Bridge,
Throwing Stones

This is the way it went: I'm leaning on the stone embankment, right about eye level with Todd's knees. Todd's throwing rocks at moving shapes in the water he says are catfish. Dan's standing up against the rail, bare legs pressed up against the rusty metal. It's hot. It's summer and we're sixteen.

Todd used to be my playmate when we were kids and he'd just moved out here from the city. We pushed matchbox cars around in the dirt, mostly. He was dumb in school and I was smart and after a year or two of being stuck in different reading groups, pushed in divergent directions by the adults around us, we gave up and caved and went where they wanted us to. Last year in tenth grade we ended up in the same art class, and once I was willing to try pot, pretending I'd done it for years, I won a friend back. Dan lived up the road from us and had been

Todd's friend all through high school. They built skateboard ramps together and went to rock concerts.

This summer we spent hanging out, smoking pot, throwing things off bridges. Dan's efforts to teach me how to stay on a skateboard failed early on, me acting like it's boring me instead of admitting I can't do it. Todd's picked up the habit of knitting these little macramé bracelets out of embroidery floss and I've got two on my left wrist, jumbled up with the band of my father's outsized Hamilton wristwatch. My father died in February.

"Can you tell me something," Todd says, watching his rock hit an alleged catfish shadow. "Are you a fag?"

This is it, I think, the question that is going to ruin my summer, the question every real boy at school asks me, usually when I'm trying to change discreetly, hidden behind my locker door, after gym, or in the hall, as they turn to knock a notebook from my hand. I should have known better than to expect different. "What?" I say, not light enough to pull it off like a joke.

"Well, the other day Dan and I were talking, and he said he bet you were." Todd's smiling this tight-lipped grin he has. Dan's face is expressionless, he's staring into the sun.

"Asshole," he says, real quiet.

I'm just staring at Todd, stern, weary of this question already, this one time more. I'm shaking too, but only a little. I'm waiting for his eyes to meet mine, but he doesn't look up. "Uh-hun," slips through my teeth.

"Is that 'uh-hun' like 'yes,' or 'uh-hun' like 'uh-huh'?" he asks, content with his trap. Lips still tightened, curled slightly. A usual expression on his face now seems full of meaning. So calm, expending so little energy to be this cruel.

"I meant 'uh-hun' like, go on, but yeah." I go for it. I'm not going to be the patsy I'm supposed to be. They can hate me for being a fag but I won't let them hate me for being a pussy. "Uh-hun. I'm a fag." I know it's still a joke. Standing up for myself now doesn't count for anything, no matter how strong I am. I thought they liked me, so the joke's on me. I'm a pussy for bearing this hurt as much as if I cried, letting it out. Still, I'm not going to give them the chance to see it.

"Okay," he says, game over.

"Why did you ask me that?" I demand.

Todd drops a handful of rocks, bunches of round wakes rippling through each other. He's my worst tormentor, leaving me to pull myself away, head home, disgraced. They'll break into laughter almost as—not after—I'm out of hearing distance.

"I'm going to go home now," I finally say, administering my own coup de grâce. Stepping up onto the bridge, I walk past Todd's back, past Dan, who regards me balefully, reaching out his hand.

"Hey, man . . ."

Pity's worse. I don't need anyone to feel sorry for me. I don't need that. "Yeah?" Cold monotone.

"I know what you're thinking—he's an asshole." He shrugs in the direction of Todd's back.

"It doesn't matter," I say.

Dan's more sensitive, doesn't like people to think bad of him. "Uhn. He's just asking that . . ."

Todd's so tickled by what a fuck he is, how successful in meanness—"heh, heh"—he's chuckling. I respect him more, maybe. More than Dan, who'd prefer to have left their fag speculations unchecked. I turn to go. I don't need to say good-bye.

"I told him last week I was gay," Dan says, holding out his empty hands. "I'm gay."

"Yeah?" I believe him. I'm more scared, feel more sick than before, feel like someone died. You wouldn't even say that as a joke, not like this anyhow.

"And he thinks it's pretty funny for some reason." I hear a few stones drop, and quiet laughter.

"Yeah, I can see that."

"Hey," Todd breaks in. "Hey, don't bitch at me."

"We were talking about people and I told him I thought probably you were too," Dan says.

"Oh." I'm not upset, or nervous. No, I am. I am both. This isn't something you talk about. This isn't something you admit to.

"The reason I think it's funny," Todd says, still raining hail on aquatic life, "is that y'all are so funny about it."

Dan kicks some gravel across the tracks, through some of the rusted-out holes. "It's not easy," he says, kind of to Todd but kind of to me too.

"Seems easy enough to me," Todd says. I used to make up stories for each of my cars, giving them personalities I'd intensify with coats of my mother's nail polish or touch-up paint from my father's toolbox; that was the game to me. Todd pushed them along, concentrating on the noise he'd make with his mouth as he forced them to navigate hairpin turns in the dirt. I didn't get it, but we played together anyhow.

"C'mon, Todd, this is weird, okay." Dan's eyes meet mine. An imaginary mirror: our first other homosexual. You think that this look might be recognition, but it's not.

I shift my gaze to Dan's feet, ratty blue high-tops cracked around the sole, him shifting his weight from toe to heel, right leg to left. "I think I'm still going to go home," I say, tilting into a stumbly walk. "I feel weird."

Dan springs forward, turning me in the opposite direction as he grabs the edge of my T-shirt sleeve. "Don't . . ." He shakes his head, upper lip shrugged over teeth. At Todd he barks, "You asshole."

Todd propels himself to his feet, pushing off the middle bar of the railing. He ambles over to us, unfazed, and walks in the direction of the road, just like we walk every day when we come back here to smoke joints. "I don't see what the big deal is," he says as we start to follow him at the same dull pace. "You want to go on forever and not ask?" He talks pointedly but at neither of us in particular, not even looking at us. "You don't ask, you never know."

"That's easy for you to say. You don't know what it's like." Dan puts his hand on the back of his neck, looking very adult. "You okay?"

I'm feeling a little better. "Yeah. I'm okay. I just want to—"

"It's not easy for me," Todd suddenly interjects, looking back over alternate shoulders at each of us in turn. "If this gets out, people are going to call me a fag lover." The severe tone contrasts with the beaming grin he's wearing, walking ahead of us down this path.

"Fag lover?" Danny snorts. "And how's it going to get out?"

"I dunno," Todd says. "Don't ask me. Y'all are the fags."

Used to Dream

I.

"I'm hungry," says Billy, clawing at my face. "You awake?" I spit hair out of my mouth. Our bed smells like piss. I'm laying in a T-shirt, my underwear lost somewhere near my ankles in the tangle of sheet. He's got one hand around my cock and the other up by my ear. "You wanna go get some pizza?"

"What time is it?" I say. He's naked, up on one elbow, looking at me, knotted reddish-brown hair hanging all in his face. "My watch is on the floor there," I say.

He reaches to pick it up by the strap. "It's one-thirty."

"In the afternoon?" I ask.

"What do you think, at night?" he says.

"You wanna fuck?" he asks.

I'm like, "I thought you were hungry."

"Oh, I am but I thought you might want to fuck first."

"Well, I don't," I say, "my ass hurts. I haven't had a solid shit in days. Because of all that fucking pizza."

"It's the perfect food," he says. "All of the food groups. Bread, dairy, vegetable, meat."

"Grease," I say.

"I thought you were tired of cooking," he says. I find a pair of underwear, pull them on. I turn on the television. "What do you want to eat, then?" Billy says.

"I don't know," I say, "why do I have to make all the decisions for everybody in the world? Why can't someone make decisions for me for a change?"

"How about a couple of bagels," Billy offers, "from the deli?"

"Would you? Get me one with butter and a slice of cheese, toasted?" He nods okay. "Well, you'll have to get out of bed to do it." He stands up, snagging a pair of jeans laying across the floor: they're the ones with no ass, just a couple calico patches held together with string. He pulls them up over his thighs, walks on his knees across the mattress to me. "Give me a kiss before I go," He says, his cock sticking out the unzipped fly. I hold it like a joystick while I kiss him, rubbing its tip with my thumb. Tucking it in with two fingers, he zips up when he stands to go. He puts on a T-shirt that was hanging over the back of a chair, grabs his brown jacket, and searches through the change on the countertop.

"Can we get one with bacon?" I ask.

"No way," he says, "we don't have enough. Besides, their bacon is a gyp. They're Jews about bacon."

My first boyfriend, Jesse, was a straight boy who killed himself to fuck with my mind. That's what he said in the note he left, half crumpled on the mattress we'd dragged together up three flights of stairs: *I never loved you: I've planned this for months: I only did this to make you feel bad.* You think I'm joking? Fine. I'm as serious as a heart attack, okay.

Anyhow, I'm over it. I'm dating Axl Rose now. William Axl: Billy. I know what you're thinking. C'mon, get real. You know better. Imagine being a sixteen-year-old hustler in West Hollywood, getting plugged by Pasadena businessmen. Guys who had to slap you around and call you a punk whore while they stuck you with their fat middle-aged cocks so they wouldn't remember their wives or their kid who was maybe about your age. Words like "fucking faggot" would fall pretty trippingly off your tongue too. Anyhow, I don't need platitudes. Billy's my boyfriend, not yours.

And he loves me too. He called me a fag the other day and I slapped his face. I mean, it's my cock he's been sucking, isn't it? And he breaks the end off this beer bottle, like you want me to stick you with this? And I'm like yeah, right, grind it into my face, you fucking queer, I'd like to see that. And he puts it down like he's gonna smile and be nice, and fucking backhands me instead. When I go to wing him back, he sits his ass right down on the glass. All of a sudden he's tears and arms around my neck and he's all sorry. I'm looking down the curve of his back, the planes of his shoulder blades and ribs, and just where it starts to curve and sprout hairs right above his ass, a couple gashes dripping red across his paste-white butt. He's holding onto me, and I'm thinking, do I trust this? I kind of don't.

One of the things I do is I go to this bar on Twelfth Street I like. I go there with my friends. Some of them I know from school, some I just know from around. Billy says I should watch how I dress when I stay out late and I say I'll dress as I please. He never worries about me when he fucks me, and that's as likely to kill me as anything else. I think he just doesn't like seeing me in a dress in the first place. It's not drag, really, just a dress. You should see me, in my beige dress with the rhinestones. In my Docs and my leather jacket. It looks nice, 'cause I've got pretty legs. I don't shave them. Don't wear makeup either. I used to want to be a girl, but just when I was real little. I mean like six.

I'm meeting my friend Dan. A school friend. He knew me when. "So you don't want to be a writer anymore?" he says.

"Well, I am," I say. "I'm writing something now."

"That's not what I mean," he says. "I mean, you should be doing something else besides . . . You have a job now?" he asks.

"Oh I got a job, you bet. I sell art supplies at Pearl Paint. Besides, it's all research," I add. I just thought of that one.

"Research?" he says, all snide. He's got a job working for a man who makes movies. "You've got a degree. Have you looked for a better job?"

"I don't need this in the slightest," I say. "Look at me, Dan. I'm a flaming fag. I've got seven earrings in my ears. I got dyed black hair down to my chin. I'm wearing a dress. Can you see me in some office somewhere?"

"Well, you could take out the earrings," he says. Then: "Never mind, it's not important, I don't mean to be an asshole."

"Besides, I help Billy with his music," I say. I really do too. I'm good at coming up with words if he's already got the music down. I wrote a couple of the songs he does.

"Well, that's something," Dan says. "You've just got to keep up with it. You can't let it stagnate, you've got real talent."

"Yeah, talent," I say. "I've got just about so much talent," I say, holding my hands about three inches apart. "Maybe more than some people, but this is New York."

"What you have to do," Dan says, "is meet people, that's how you get places. You let them see how good you are, and they'll help you out."

"Maybe when I'm forty," I say. "I'm no child prodigy or anything. Maybe I thought I was once, in a different place. It's easier to be smarter than a bunch of dumb kids in high school. It's hard to be smart on your own."

"Life's hard," he says, "but Art's fun. Vita brevis and all."

"Oh, bullshit, absolutely don't start with that crap. It's life that's easy. I don't even think about it. But Art . . . man, I'm writing something, and it's even good, maybe, and I'm listening to a tape while I do it, and some line, one stupid line, will jump out of the song to tell me I'm a loser, that I'm never going to be able to write anything that'll make people feel something."

"Like what line?" he asks.

I know them by heart, these fucking lines from pop songs that hang around my neck like millstones: Marianne Faithfull singing Dylan's "I'll Keep It with Mine," or Nico, doing the same. Searching for something that's not lost. Approaching fifty, Nico got off drugs and got hit by a truck riding her bike down the street.

"It's not just the lines, it's the music that really gets you. That's why I like helping Billy. But even that doesn't seem as good to me."

Dan's on his third Rolling Rock and I can sense he's getting a little uneasy around me. "You look at me thinking what went wrong," I say.

"No, not what went wrong." He kind of shakes his head, leaning it on one shoulder. "That's what happens when they send you to these artsy-fartsy schools. You don't really learn how to do anything except stuff that people don't need. It's a perfect education, as long as you grow up to be famous."

"I haven't given up on that," I say, though I think we're talking about two entirely different things. "It takes more time than you'd think. Lots of great artists didn't make it big until their forties. Most, I'd say. Oscar Wilde. Beethoven, Dennis Cooper," I say.

"Oh, he's not in his forties," Dan says.

"Close enough," I say. "Too old to be writing about punk teenagers."

"I met him once," Dan says.

"You didn't," I say. I mean that. I don't believe him.

"Yeah, I did too. The guy I work for was friends with him when he lived in New York."

"Why does he write those stories?" I ask. "All those stories about teenage boys getting chopped up. You think he beats up his boyfriend?"

Dan's annoyed. "It's about alienation. The dehumanization of modern culture. Why do you play dumb?" He goes to the bar, gets two more beers. I'm not dumb. I prefer to take things literally. Anyhow, alienation's a stupid-ass thing to write a story about. I can't believe anyone would go to the trouble.

"Dan," I say, "don't get pissed, I'm not trying to stiff you. I'm completely broke."

"I got it," he says, "don't worry about it. You're smoking like a fiend."

"Am I?" I say. We've both been smoking from my pack and there's like three left. "Yeah, you're right." I tap out two onto the table, one for me, one for him.

"You still living with that junkie?"

"C'mon Dan," I say, lighting my cig. "We've been over this."

"I just worry about you, man."

"We both used to do a lot of coke and that can give you a heart attack. We're both drunk. We're both chain-smoking."

"As long as you're okay with it," he says. It gets like this; he's watching me like he's real, real sorry for me, like he knows something I don't.

"You're starting to act like my dad," I say.

"So what is it that you're writing anyhow?" he says.

"What I'm doing now," I say, "is I'm preparing the unauthorized biography of Axl Rose."

"Are you now?"

"Billy's probably starting to worry," I say, even though he doesn't.

"Want me to walk you back? It's on the way. I've got to catch the Green Line."

"Nah," I say. "No, I'm okay." I leave him sitting there. I'm about three blocks away, halfway home, when I stop into the deli and buy myself a new pack of cigarettes and a forty-ouncer.

Billy says, "I'm in here," when I pull on the bathroom door. It's locked. "I know what's going on here," I say, banging on the door. "All right, mister," I say, "open up."

Switching the latch from his seat on the toilet, Billy pulls the door open a crack, enough for me to see his face. "What? I'm on the toilet." And I ask why is the door locked if he's just taking a shit. He says, "Maybe I just felt like taking a shit with the door locked."

He narrows the crack again, and when I hear the latch click, I smack the door with my open palm.

He takes a slug of my beer when he comes out finally, tugging the left arm of his long underwear shirt way down over the crook of his elbow, like I'm too stupid to know where track marks are. He looks up at me. "What's the matter," he asks me with vomit breath, "what are you being a bitch about now?"

"What do you mean, what's the matter, you asshole?" I say. "You think I'm retarded in the brain?"

"Nuh-un," he says, "I'm not on junk, man. It's always the same with you, isn't it? You have to know what I'm doing every fucking second."

"Don't you have anything else to do besides sit around on your lazy ass shooting up? Aren't you supposed to be some sort of musician or something?" I say.

And he says, "Don't you have anything better to do than get up my ass?"

"I used to be a nice boy. People used to say I had a future. Then I met you." That's what I say to him. He's just sitting there picking strange crud out from underneath his fingernails. "Aren't you even going to look at me when I'm talking?" I say.

"I'm getting a new tattoo," he says to my back as I turn away from him, fixing my gaze out the window. "I'm getting a big red Q right over my heart with your initials in it. 'Cause I'm queer for you, baby."

"And what're you gonna do when we break up finally?" I ask.

"I'll run it through with a big black line and put the next guy's initials underneath."

There's a bunch of Puerto Rican kids hanging out in the light of a stoop across the street. There's a gray dog tied to the fence and one of the kids is making him bark. He knows how long the leash is, and is standing right at the place where the tip of the dog's nose reaches. He grabs the dog by the snoot and shakes its head and laughs. The dog jumps and snaps its jaws. The boy leans his head in, making noises back at it. He squats down, rests his hands on the knees of his khakis, curling his lip at the dog. The dog's not really mad. I can see that. It's the boy's dog.

"You're getting lost out there," says the asshole on the couch. "Baby, why don't you sit down here with me?"

"Oh, Billy man. Are you gonna stop this?" I say.

"I only did a little. The first time in days almost. My legs were twitching."

"This isn't why I went to college," I tell him.

"Put your head on my stomach," he says.

II.

Billy and I are lying down watching the television. I'm upright at one end of the couch, with Billy stretched out between my legs, his head on my folded arms. The news is on, and down in Killeen, Texas, some guy has just driven his car through the front window of Luby's cafeteria and shot a whole bunch of people. He must have been something else because his neighbors didn't act like the usual mass murderer's neighbors. The lady next door told the TV reporter in a confident voice: "He was crazy. I always knew he'd pull something like this one day."

Maybe the people who say, "He was a nice guy, kept to himself mostly," just don't know the signs to look for. Personally, I think I'd notice a guy dressing in fatigues, collecting military-style riflery, and barricading his house with high fences and shrubbery.

Billy snorts, shaking his head, "No. If that were true, every adult man and three-fifths of the teenagers in West Texas would be mass murderers."

"The way you talk about it sounds like they were."

"No. Not mass murderers," he says, flipping the channel with the remote. "Just rednecks."

"I grew up in the country," I say, mildly annoyed.

"Humph," Billy says.

"You know I did," I repeat, shoving him off me. He catches himself from falling by bracing against the floor with one arm. When I say, "Fuck you," he cracks up and, laughing, rolls to the floor with a thud.

He sits up on the carpet, spitting strands of hair away from his face, still giggling. "Where you come from," he says, "doesn't count. You grew up in a fucking Norman Rockwell painting."

Which is actually more or less true. When I say "country" I mean a place with fields and cows and trees. Creeks spanned by one-lane bridges with green railings. I have seen pictures of where Billy grew up. With all that big, deserty space spreading to the horizon, you wonder why they build the houses three yards from the highway.

The city and the country are similar enough, is what I've discovered in the five years since I moved to New York. I think Billy and I both feel pretty much at home. You go to the grocery store and the clerk knows what you want. You say hi to your neighbors on their stoops. It's the suburbans I don't get, their half-communal, half-defensive mind-set a complete mystery. When they live in the city they go to every bodega within a five-block radius just so the clerk won't get to know their habits. They like having dozens of acquaintances they hate and they like to gossip. Most of my friends grew up suburban and they like to say things like, "I hope you aren't being sucked into paying his way," and "Maybe you're like my friend Jodie. She doesn't think she deserves to be happy," or "I'd just think you'd like being with someone who shared your interests."

My friends and I read a lot. Reading is an interest. Every time I go to a party, in the Village or in Soho or in Park Slope, I look at bookshelves. I have found five titles which everyone in the whole world who's been to college in the last three years has copies of, even if the spines aren't always cracked. When I want Billy to read *Discipline and Punish* or *Gravity's Rainbow*, I'll know where to find copies.

Billy's favorite book is the dictionary. It's how he learned most everything he knows, having finished with school when he ran away from home at fifteen. The best one, he says, is the one with essays in the front, one by William F. Buckley, who admits maybe that language can change theoretically, but that rules must be obeyed until the right people decide otherwise, and another by a guy who says Buckley's full of shit, that we can't do anything but study and write and think about the ways people use their language. That using it makes it real. Whatever people do is real. This is what Billy agrees with, and he talks about William F. Buckley sometimes as if he were a very persuasive and dangerous man. Purely because of his dictionary essays, not because of the tattoos he wants on our asses and on Billy's left arm.

I guess I took words for granted because all I ever did with a dictionary when I was a kid was look up dirty words. Sexual words like "penis," "vagina," slang terms like "shit," "fuck," "asshole." Words with secondary dirty meanings like "cock" or "dick" or "screw" with lines of stuffy definitions—"Booby: 1. a species of aquatic fishing birds, usually black-feathered"—before they'd finally concede "a woman's mammary." "Hump" was my favorite: "(offensive slang) to copulate." "Hump" means to have sex like a dog and sweat and grunt. Hey, Billy, wanna hump?

When I was a kid all I fantasized about was what my life would be like when I made all this money. I guess that's normal. No kid fantasizes about working hard, coming home with a headache, taking a nap, then watching TV before initiating some perfunctory sex. I never dreamed about walking down a city street at four-thirty in the morning, drunk with bloody snot balling up in my nose holes. Who knew there were reasons to get so fucked up?

I asked Billy what his childhood fantasies were, once. More practical than mine, I guess, depending on what you think fantasies are for. "I used to dream," he said, "that one day I'd be big enough to kick my dad's ass."

"I have issues." I remember telling my friend Dan that Billy had said that to me, early on, the first week he was staying at my place. He wouldn't remove his clothes with the lights on. He pretended to fall asleep while we watched Letterman, and I guess I was supposed to touch him then. He had to move my hand onto him.

"He has issues!" Dan rolled his eyes with delight. "That's cute."

Billy was the most beautiful boy I had ever slept with. It didn't bother me that no one else could see it. Beneath the dirty black clothes he wore his skin was cool and smooth, the color of milk; beneath his defiantly tangled long hair he had the face of a Renaissance Gabriel. "I like issues," I said.

After two weeks, Billy took off his shirt so I could put it in the laundry. A number of dense, straight white scars ran from his stomach to underneath the waistband of his sweatpants. I touched one, imagining he might flinch. Instead he said, "I like you. I really like you. But some things are none of your business."

He used that line a lot. None of my business: where he was the night before when he said he'd be home at seven but didn't come home till twelve, obviously fucked up. "I wasn't screwing anyone else, okay?" What happened to the twenty bucks I gave him yesterday. When he got that card for the Needle Exchange. None of my business.

"Was he like a strict disciplinarian? Was it spanking or was it hitting? Did your mother try to stop him?"

Some things are super none of my business. "What is it? You want hillbilly stories with a woodshed out back? Why don't you let it drop?"

"My dad had an alcohol problem too. Billy, it's not like we're so different."

"Listen." He seriously leaned into my face, startling me. "I don't fucking want to hear about we're not so different." I stepped back, gasped. I guess maybe I snorted. He didn't like the sound of it. "If I smacked you now you'd fucking remember it for a long time."

The doorway where Billy and I first had sex is only about two blocks from where we live now. I got a bloody knee from the broken glass in front of him. He gripped me by the hair above the neck. Shoulders pressed against the brick wall, he arched his back. "Yeah, get me off, cocksucker." I stood when he let me loose, my numbed nose dripping. He laughed and I was scared. Then he grabbed my head again, pulling me toward him, and sucked his sperm out of my mouth.

Three and a half years ago now. We're in love now, so sex is different. We know what to expect, mostly. Jack off and go to sleep mostly. We even eat brunch now. There are occasional bursts of excitement. "I am an ugly piece of shit with nothing going on and you are a sick fuck for wanting to have sex with me," or "You're getting fat, when you sit on my dick you crush all my guts and I can't breathe."

"I love you," I protest, slobbering over him and prolonging the act forever. When we used to use rubbers, sometimes he'd stay in so long afterwards the thing would come off in my ass.

I still feel like I want to know everything about him. I hate that there are things still off-limits. I'm leaning against the sink in our bathroom brushing my teeth, watching Billy take a shit. We can do that now. It doesn't bother us. It's not supposed to.

I spit out the foam and slurp some cold water directly out of the faucet. But instead of leaving then, I decide to stay and see how Billy's project turns out. "Tell me what it feels like," I say.

He's sitting limply forward on the pot, his hands dangling together between his knees. The reddish hair on his shins is bristling, standing on end above the inside-out legs of the jeans pooled around his ankles. "You're a freak."

"How's it feel?" I repeat. "Big? Small? Is it going to come out in one log, or two? Clean or greasy?"

"It's soft," he says, eyes closed, like a medium channeling a hesitant spirit. "I'm going to try and push out all I can. It'll need wiping."

"No it won't," I say. "You're not going to wipe it."

I kneel down on the linoleum in front of him, resting my hands on his naked thighs. I stare up at his face. He's keeping his eyes sort of closed but I see a flicker of iris through the pale lashes. Grabbing his cock and balls, I lift them to one side so I can see the poop coming out.

"Don't it feel good up there? A cock feels better than that, even."

"Stop," he says. "You're getting me hard." The poop breaks off, splashing water on the underside of Billy's legs; on my chin.

"I want to pee on you," I say.

"No," he says. "Don't. I mean it."

"Just a little."

"Don't."

"I'll just aim between your legs, all right?" He doesn't

answer me, so I kick my shoes off against the side of the tub, pull down my pants and underpants, taking them off by standing on one leg with one foot, extracting the other, then repeating. Naked from the waist down, I sit across Billy's lap and direct a stream of piss towards his dick. It ricochets onto his legs, his pubic hair, the tails of our shirts. He slides his hands up my chest, underneath my T-shirt, and exposes one of my nipples for him to chew on. His dick brushes my leg as it comes to life on its own for once. "It's alive," I say, and he laughs, and says, "I'm gonna fuck you in the ass," because we've talked about it and agreed that fucking "in" the ass is dirtier than fucking "up" the ass.

"I'm gonna fuck you in the ass," he repeats as he pulls my chest to his face, drumming his fingertips along my butt crack. He scowls and winces as the toilet handle pokes him in the back, and I have to brace myself against the sink to keep from falling off.

"You're an idiot," I say. He'd been trying to pee on my ass and missed so I bite his throat, stand up on the slippery floor, and poke my dick at his mouth. He refuses to take it, shaking his head no so his bottom lip rubs me the way I like. "Suck it, bitch."

"You're the bitch," he says with two fingers inside me.

I know this boy from the inside out. I've felt the rumble of an unborn fart travel inside his body and the pulse of the pale blue veins glistening under his thin skin. How he works beyond the physical I don't even pretend to know.

"This is the way our relationship's gonna end: you're gonna walk out on me, and I'm going to hunt you down and kidnap you and bring you back here and stab you, and while I'm watching you bleed to death, I'm going to shoot myself in the head," Billy says to me after we've exhausted ourselves fucking. "Or else, you're gonna have to kill me. I'll be fucked up and come at you and you won't have a choice."

"You're only saying that because you love me," I tell him. "You won't always think I'm worth killing."

Smoking cigarettes afterwards, drinking coffee in the kitchen: "I've been lying to you," he says.

"About the heroin?" He told me he's stopped. I know he hasn't, but he's been trying. He's been copping methadone off the street but sometimes you can't find it.

He shakes his head. "They got infected," he says. "My scars. I did it with a razor blade. They weren't that deep. I guess I couldn't stop picking at them."

He sighs and lets his hair fall into his face, turns away slightly and with exacting casualness performs the act of refilling his coffee cup from the pot on the stove.

"I didn't run away because my dad hit me," he says.

And one night he whispers in my ear, "Would you want to fuck me? I mean, should we try?" I let my hand drop from the small of his back to the cleft of his butt.

"It hurts," he says, when I spread his legs and get in between them, pressing my way in.

"I'll stop."

"No, please don't." I keep my weight off him as best I can and try to slide it in gently. He looks at me timidly, nodding his assent. I lay down on top of him and poke it all the way home and he gasps, horrified. Cringing.

"Billy," I say, pulling out. His hands dig into my shoulder blades, legs locked around my back. "No. Stay in. I want you to."

I don't dare move, hard inside him as he breathes heavily into the side of my face. "Oh, Christ," he mutters. "Jesus fuck."

Billy is crying.

"You're the only man that's done this to me, do you understand? No one else ever. I saved this for you my whole life."

My Billy boy.

He says, "This erases everything else, okay?"

Selected Lives in Brief

Mark Findlay

At age twenty-four, Mark Findlay was a part-time bartender at an Irish bar, Mike Riley's, on First Avenue in New York City's East Village. He worked Tuesday and Wednesday nights, Sunday afternoons, and Fridays as the secondary bartender on duty. He had shoulder-length reddish-brown hair and because of him college girls and other young people started to come to the bar to drink, play pool, and play the jukebox. Before this, Mike Riley's had been sort of an old-fashioned neighborhood bar with an older, working-class male crowd. Mark had been permitted by his boss to select music for the jukebox, and he had gotten some Pogues, Clash, U2, and other popular music onto it. He was amiable and considered good-looking, though mostly because of his accent, which was fairly rare among young guys. Mark was from Ireland. He lived in Yonkers with his uncle but eventually got an apartment on East Twelfth Street.

Mark liked to mix odd drinks, but because young people did not like to drink so many odd cocktails he would sometimes invent them fancifully while his fans played pool and then offer what he had made to them for free. This was an acceptable business strategy because it made these kids like the bar and also to drink with abandon, forgetting that they were, in fact, paying good money for at least three-quarters of what they were drinking. He was also tipped very well. Sometimes he had to pay himself for the free drinks he made if he had used expensive liquors to make them.

Once he had an apartment in the East Village, Mark would go out drinking to other bars where some of the relief bartenders also worked, or places the kids who came to his bar went drinking on other nights. Sometimes he would go out to see bands play, because he was often invited by band members to come see their bands.

One Saturday night he was hanging out with a small group of kids drinking beer after a band had played and they all decided to go back to someone's apartment and snort some coke. Mark was thought to be very funny. He pretended to get all crazy on coke and pretend-fought with some of the other boys. He made a subsequent beer run with one of the boys, a kid named Doug, and Doug thought maybe Mark was being flirty on their walk, but, as this flirtiness was only a matter of eye contact and an ambiguous smiling, Doug did not regard it with any certainty. It had not occurred to him that Mark could be gay and he didn't know Mark well enough to have been that comfortable making it clear that he himself was gay. Doug did not hang around all that much with gay guys and often the straight guys his friends were friends with did not pick up on him being gay. But he liked Mark smiling at him and Mark always gave him every third drink free so he enjoyed this attention a little more than he would have with another random straight guy.

When the apartment party was winding down, Doug and Mark ended up walking home together. They bought slices of pizza on St. Mark's and more beer at the corner deli and sat on a stoop talking and drinking. Mark said that there was something about himself that he did not tell people, especially his young friends from the bar, because people might not understand and might not think well of him if they knew what his secret was. Doug thought he guessed what Mark was talking about. They were sitting in a peculiar way—Doug on a step midway up the stoop with his legs spread, forty-ouncer of beer by his side, Mark a few steps down, leaning back against the inside of Doug's leg, pressing back harder every time he reached for the beer. After a while, they wandered back toward Mark's apartment and stood, awkwardly, in front of the building for a while, talking bullshit, Doug very awkward and Mark smiling and blushing.

They kissed once on the lips, chastely, briefly and afraid. Then they kissed, for a while, like two people who were going to have sex, their arms around each other's chest and shoulders, their tongues in each other's mouth, the hardening bulges in their jeans rubbing together electrically. Mark stopped to say he could not let Doug come up to his apartment and, after more kissing, Doug told him they could go to his. Without taking his warm hand off Doug's back, Mark said he had to go upstairs and sleep, had to get up the next day, but he would see Doug around, surely. Doug felt weird and anxious walking the rest of the block to Avenue A. The few people loitering around the street may have noticed he was one of two boys kissing on the street. But maybe, because of Mark's hair, they had not noticed he was a boy. Or maybe they did not see, or maybe care.

Doug was very upset by what had happened. He thought he had somehow done something wrong, or else that Mark was not sure of his sexuality and that kissing him might cause ill effects somewhere down the road.

———

In fact, Mark could not let Doug upstairs because he had a lot of guns in his apartment that weekend. He had eight semiautomatic rifles lying underneath a plaid flannel sheet on his couch, and several boxes of ammunition as well. He needed to wrap them and pack them into cardboard boxes the next morning so that associates of his uncle could pick them up and ship them out in whatever strange way they had of shipping such things out. He was going to accept two thousand dollars in cash for them and put half of it into his own bank account and take the other half up to his uncle in Yonkers and be done with it all by one o'clock in the afternoon when his Sunday shift at Mike Riley's started. Since it was four-thirty A.M. already, Mark was worried about how tired he'd be. He set his alarm for seven-thirty, lay in bed, masturbated thinking about Doug, and took his short night's sleep.

Mark had emigrated illegally at age seventeen, partly to assist in his uncle's IRA activity and partly because he had always wanted to leave Belfast and live in America. As a bartender he had sometimes allowed himself to be drawn into discussions about Ireland and he was not easily able to repress his opinion but he tried to keep his responses general. This was difficult when he was angry or drunk. Americans did not often understand that it did not matter if the British government was generally democratic or humanitarian or that they no longer enforced discrimination against Catholics; that the violence Americans knew of was almost always attributed to the IRA. The point was, quite simply, that the British had conquered another country and sent their citizens to live there and was now pretending that those citizens were just as Irish as anyone and had a right to self-determination, which meant that his country could be ruled by the British and the British could defend their rule by placing armed soldiers on every street corner of the neighborhood he grew up in—and they could call this democracy and every other civilized nation would pretend that it was, just in order to get along. Even though they knew what kind of imperialists the British were and recognized the rights of people to fight them in Africa and Asia and America and every other place imperialists were no longer wanted by the people they had ruled.

This was, in any case, what Mark felt, and as openly as he would express himself when compelled to say something about it. If anyone should talk about the monstrous rich ignoramuses in Boston or New York who gave money to buy implements of death solely out of some half-remembered asserted loyalty to the shillelagh and the shamrock, Mark would instantly clam the fuck up and shake his head and say he didn't know, it was all terrible.

The next time this boy Doug came into the bar, he was very shy and would not stray very far from his friends. Mark tried to be very friendly and encouraging to him when he came to the bar to buy their drinks but Doug had been somewhat scared off by being sent home alone. After his friends had grown too drunk to play pool well and the crowd had thinned out, they all wandered over to the bar and chose stools and slumped over their drinks. Mark asked for one of Doug's cigarettes even though he had his own and leaned in to ask Doug to light it even though he had his own lighter. He wrote his phone number down on a napkin right in front of Doug and slid it to him and said, "I hope you'll call me." Doug took it, somewhat confused, and put it into his pocket.

Paul Honishiro

Paul Honishiro grew up in Silver Spring, Maryland, and Glendale, Maryland. He was born in 1964. His father was an engineer for Martin Marietta. He had an older sister and a younger sister. His mother was a moderately religious Protestant. His father told stories sometimes about having been in an internment camp in California in the forties, when he would have been seven and eight. His mother was a very self-sufficient type who believed that anyone could achieve what they worked for in America. She leaned towards Republican politics and liked Ronald Reagan. His father earned good money and voted for local Republican politicians who promised low property taxes and good schools, but he remained wary of American-dream-type politics because of what he remembered being done to his parents and himself during World War II.

Paul was in accelerated programs for the gifted in mathematics while he was in public elementary school. He was good at math but it gave him a headache. He preferred playing Little League softball and soccer to doing schoolwork. Sometimes the parents of his friends would ask him where his family came from and Paul would tell them San Jose, California, which was where his grandparents lived and his father had grown up. This was not what anyone meant by asking, but he kept answering with this response even when he was old enough to know what they meant. His father had gone to Stanford University, and his older sister wanted to go there too and study medicine. His mother, however, valued and praised Paul's interest in sports. She took it as a sign of Americanness and felt, on some level, a

need for her family to distinguish itself from the more relentlessly academic grasping which she associated with Asian immigrant types. Mrs. Honishiro was somewhat of a snob. Paul grew into a large adolescent, almost six foot and one hundred seventy pounds at age fourteen. He got a spot on the junior varsity lacrosse team at his high school and was the youngest boy on the team. His grandparents called him their jock and his grandfather asked him about girlfriends, of which Paul had none.

Paul's high school was not very racially diverse but he did not notice this much. He was the only Asian boy among the preppie jock clique—the boys who played soccer in the fall and lacrosse in the spring and whichever sport in the winter they were good at, basketball or wrestling. Paul did not go out for wrestling because he had wrestled in gym class and the position of having your crotch pressed up against another boy's butt filled him with anxiety and dread. So Paul went out for basketball instead. He was popular and had many friends. Many girls liked him and would hang out with him and his friends at the mall or at school after games, but he did not often place himself in dating-type positions.

One girl in particular, Kelly Burckholder, was a good friend and when Paul needed to go to a school dance with a girl he would go with Kelly and not even have to ask, really. Kelly was a big-boned preppie blond girl who played field hockey and basketball and girl's lacrosse, though their junior year she was coaxed to pitch for the softball team and that year they won the state championship. Paul and Kelly did not kiss or feel each other up when they were alone. They went to parties together and drank beer and told each other funny stories when other people stopped paying attention to them because everyone was drunk or gone off to make out.

That same year as he started drinking beer and going to parties, Paul started to like a boy, and he knew he would have liked to have sex with this boy but did not see how it was possible, so he did not pursue it except as a friendship. This boy was a foreign exchange student from Spain with sculpted cheekbones and little muscles or spit glands that bulged slightly at his jawline. He liked soccer a good deal. They would practice together, their sweaty shirts off, stuffed into the elastic of their gym shorts, from which they hung like tails. By age sixteen Paul had soft, straight black hair in a line up his stomach and right around his nipples; he had this hair at the small of his back. His Spanish friend would say that Japanese people weren't supposed to have body hair and Paul would say, "Well, I do." And his Spanish friend would say that Japanese people were supposed to have smaller dicks and Paul would say, "Not as small as yours, I bet."

But Paul did not have a small dick and his Spanish friend didn't either, except Paul noticed his friend's foreskin with some interest in the locker room. No one had foreskins so all the guys noticed it. The Spanish friend was not embarrassed or shy about showing it off a little. Sometimes he would even touch it, not to get it hard or anything sexual but like it was just a part of his body it would be strange and odd to avoid touching while showering or drying. Which was not what American boys like Paul felt about their dicks. Masturbating was something dirty to do in secret and when you pissed in a urinal you barely did more than pinch some loose skin to pull your dick out of the fly of your boxers and make sure it was aimed right. In the shower at school you might accidentally brush your hand against it while soaping your stomach but you would never lather up your hand and roll your dick in your palm. Which is what Paul's Spanish friend did when he took a shower after practice.

Paul ended up telling Kelly Burckholder about his friend's uncircumcised dick and this led Kelly to ask about Paul's dick and this led to Paul and Kelly performing an act of sexual intercourse. Neither of them looked too closely at the other's genitals but they managed fine. Paul's dick would not stay all that hard and he found himself thinking of his Spanish friend and the bodies of other boys so he figured, "Oh, well. I guess I really must be a fag or something." Paul did not want to be a fag. He wanted to like Kelly. They went to the homecoming dance together as seniors and they were elected the King and Queen of Homecoming. They went to the prom together later that year. Kelly applied to and was accepted to Bryn Mawr, Goucher, St. Mary's, and William and Mary, and after talking about it with her friends and family and Paul, she chose Bryn Mawr. Paul applied to and was accepted to U.Va, William and Mary, Towson State, and the University of Maryland, and he decided to go to William and Mary. He had also applied to Stanford to mollify his father but he did not get in. He also did not get into Johns Hopkins University.

———

In college, Paul continued to date Kelly for his freshman year. It was useful to have a pretty, jocky girlfriend to have pictures of but who was not around very often. It kept people from setting him up or hitting on him or wondering why he didn't date more. Paul declared his major as political science and played on the lacrosse team, but there were better athletes than him for the soccer team and the basketball team, and most of the basketball players were black. Paul's roommate at college was a blond white boy from Virginia who sometimes had sex in their room with Paul supposedly asleep. For a while they always ate together and went to parties together, but second semester this roommate made some additional friends, which subtracted from his and Paul's hang-out time. One time Paul got very upset over this and almost cried. His roommate knew he was trying not to cry when Paul explained that he had thought they were very close. He thought Paul was being overly emotional, which was not a quality a person saw much in Paul.

Once Paul recognized he had been doing this overly emotional thing, he tried his best to force it back down inside himself. From then on he was cool but friendly to his roommate, and began drinking more heavily with some of his lacrosse friends and political science friends. One time he was very drunk and asked an acquaintance named Tom—to whom Paul imagined he was much closer, emotionally, then he in fact was—if he had ever thought about messing around with a guy. Tom was drunk also and very reluctantly admitted he had. They got drunker and passed out but didn't have sex. A few weeks later Paul did not think of Tom a lot anymore and only saw him around. Paul got a job for the summer as a counselor at a sports camp and he stayed in Virginia Beach in a cramped apartment he shared with four other guys from his dorm.

Early in the semester of his sophomore year, Paul's father called to tell him that he had been diagnosed with pancreatic cancer. Though his mother and sister tried to dissuade him from quitting school and moving back home, Paul did this anyway. He got a job at a local sporting goods store and stayed home with his dad a lot while trying to work a transfer to the University of Maryland. His father died in the spring and Paul secured his enrollment at the University of Maryland and switched his major from political science to business administration. He had transferred in too late to go out for the lacrosse team there but he met guys who had an informal sports club and drank and played rough preppie sports. Paul joined them.

Paul was able to get a decent discount on some rugby shirts for the group from the store he continued to work part-time at. It occurred to him that there was some demand for group orders of sports equipment on a smaller scale than a school athletic department but nevertheless in enough volume to cut deals with custom manufacturers and reap an attractive profit. One of the guys in the sports club, Eric, had some offhand design experience and helped Paul create some logos and motifs for a line of sports clothing. Paul contacted some of the local equipment manufacturers and put together a mail-order newsletter that he marketed towards socially geared sports organizations on college campuses. The living room of his apartment in College Park was soon crowded with boxes of clothes and boxes of catalog material.

Paul began to be curious about Eric, his design-oriented friend from the sports club who seemed to have a natural flair for striking color combinations and was proving very useful for his enterprise. First Paul made Eric a one-quarter partner in his new business and second Paul went out drinking in George-town with Eric and at a certain point asked him if he had ever thought about messing around with a guy. Eric was drunk also and reluctantly admitted, yes, in fact he was gay and he hoped that Paul could deal with it and accept him because it didn't, after all, mean that much. Paul told Eric that he thought, too, sometimes, that he might be bisexual or gay but that he just didn't know if it was something he could explore. Eric shrugged. Eric knew that straight guys said things like that.

Paul graduated college with a business degree in 1986. He and Eric expanded the catalog distribution and Paul encouraged Eric to design more fabrics and clothes. In 1988 they opened their first store in the Columbia Mall and by 1991 they had three stores in the D.C. area. In 1992 he struck a deal with Barnes and Noble about them carrying his gear at the increas-ing number of college bookstores they operated. By then Eric had found himself a boyfriend and at least in private Paul was almost comfortable enough to say that he also was gay. Paul and Eric were profiled in *Washington Magazine's* 1993 issue of young entrepreneurs and Paul was also honored by being put on their Top 50 Bachelors list. The list made it sound like Paul was straight.

That July he went to the gay March on Washington with Eric and he saw some people he had been at school with at

William and Mary. Paul thought he saw Kelly Burckholder but the woman was a long distance away and he couldn't really call out to her. It would make some sense if it was her, though, Paul thought. And then he wouldn't feel so bad about having treated her like he did.

As he approached thirty, Paul began to feel self-conscious about his body, which could still run and jump and stuff but sagged more than it had. He had always been sort of thick-waisted but his fat used to be adolescent-looking and resilient—and now he was starting to look like an aging beer-swilling jock. Which is what he was, after all. He did not look as sharp as he would wish, considering that he was often photographed playing sports and these images were associated with his own clothing and sporting goods line. He decided, for reasons he considered purely practical, to start a heavy-duty workout program, and Eric's boyfriend suggested an athletic club he thought would suit Paul well.

Eric's boyfriend worked out with Paul at this athletic club, and often afterwards Eric would meet them and they would eat dinner together. Paul liked Eric's boyfriend very much as a friend, which made him realize rather suddenly that Eric was his best friend and had been his best friend for ten years. Paul had never felt goofy or uneasy or self-conscious about being around Eric; he had never moped around wondering how close they were or how much Eric really liked him. So he had not noticed until then how much he loved Eric and how much Eric loved him. But when he did notice this it made him happy.

By late 1996, Paul's company was praised by the *Wall Street Journal* for its early and astute use of the World Wide Web in marketing its products. He was far from being a millionaire personally but his company had over two million dollars in assets. His body looked great and he had washboard abs for the first time in his life. He was photographed with no shirt on for a spread in the *Washington Post*'s Sunday magazine, skin darkened from his last trip to Bermuda, bright red and blue war paint slashing his cheeks and chest. Paul drove a metallic-brown Saab convertible and dated men. He wasn't sure what he wanted in a man, though. He'd told his sister but he wondered how his mom would take it if he ever found a guy he really liked and wanted to live with. He wondered what his dad would have thought about any of it: the business, his being gay, Eric.

Darin Brock Holloway

Darin Brock Holloway was born on May 3, 1971, in Lenox, Massachusetts, but his parents were from Long Island in New York and they moved back there when he was still a baby. There was nothing about him as a baby that would have made you think he would grow up to star in pornographic movies for homosexuals. I don't know what there would be about any baby to make a normal person think such a thing. But the case is, that's what he grew up to be, so this is the kind of childhood such a person may have.

Sometimes he had to stay with his grandparents at their apartment complex. There was a small playground to one side with fiberglass rocking animals for children to ride. There was a red pony and a green lizard and an orange sea horse. Darin, as he was called then, liked the orange sea horse best. His grandmother wore her hair pulled back in a bun and used coral-colored lipstick and Tigress powder, which sat on the bathroom vanity in a cylindrical container with a black bottom part and a tiger-patterned upper part. The tiger-patterned upper part was goldish instead of tiger orange, and it had a tassel. Darin's mother used a spray bottle of Coty that did not seem peculiar or mysterious to him. The Tigress powder did seem both peculiar and mysterious. His grandfather died when he was too young to hold memories very well, and after he was six or seven he did not stay so often at his grandparents'.

Darin's father drank but did not abuse him much. Darin's father was a groundskeeper for a high school near where they lived in Long Island, and his mother drove a school bus. Darin did not mind this when he was in elementary school but he began to mind it later, once he was old enough to have to go to school where his parents worked. But before that, he had an aunt who was killed in a car accident and that summer his two cousins came to stay while his uncle traveled to California to get settled in a new job. His cousins were both male and both older than him, though not by many years. They would play war, and the way they played war often ended with all three boys lying in bed naked, acting hurt and ill. By the end of the summer his oldest cousin had grown to dislike this game and to be ashamed of it, even though all they did was be naked and act hurt.

When his cousins left for California and Darin began sixth grade, he had trouble getting along with other children. He had straight blond hair that his mother cut in a bowl style. He was aggressive and not a very good learner. He smoked his first cigarette then and shortly afterwards his first marijuana cigarette, which an older boy had offered him. This older boy lived in his neighborhood and was perceived to be somewhat responsible—he mowed lawns and worked on an old car. He would baby-sit for Darin's parents sometimes. This boy was sixteen and Darin was twelve. He masturbated Darin and taught Darin to masturbate him. Once he fellated Darin briefly but would not permit Darin to fellate him back. He took Darin to the YMCA and encouraged him in swimming. Darin fell in love with him but though he admired Darin's determination and rigid little body he did not love Darin back because Darin was a child.

———

When Darin started at the high school where his father worked, he grew angry at his parents' constant scrutiny and began to socialize with older, bad kids he knew his parents would not like. He began to play hooky, and take drugs. He had sex with girls but never enjoyed it very much for its own sake. He had one friend with whom he would pursue girls and occasionally they had sex with the same girl at almost the same time and Darin could perform quite well in that situation.

When he was fifteen a man offered him money to visit with him. He had been standing around the strip shopping mall waiting for his friend but instead this man approached. Darin went with him and was fellated and received twenty dollars. When the man drove him back to the shopping center, he gave the man his telephone number. Darin's father was angry when the man called the house, and did not believe Darin's explanations.

Within a few months, more than one man had called the house and Darin's father had become very angry. He beat Darin and tried to spank him but Darin said something to his father which made him too embarrassed and too livid to spank him. Instead his father simply made him leave the house. He was happy to do so. He ran away to New York City, which was one and a half hours away by train. It was not easy to find men to pay you money for sex there unless you were willing to stand around places Darin did not feel comfortable standing around. But he did find other young people who had run away and some of these were nice to him. He found a girlfriend even though he did not want one. He would have preferred a boyfriend but boys did not offer to take care of you the way girls did, even when they enjoyed your friendship and had sex with you.

———

Darin renamed himself Brock and traveled with his new girl-friend to Hollywood. They would relax on a street corner and play a transistor radio and dance and sometimes men would walk by and say something to the girl and sometimes they would say something to Brock. They would leave with these men and meet up later to eat—at a cheap diner or out of a Dumpster—and the stories they most preferred to tell were about the nice apartments they'd seen and how these men were so sad and lonely and nice that all they had done was sat and talked with them. This was true sometimes. They both got ugly tattoos during this time, but the designs meant something symbolic to each of them, even though they had just picked them off sheets at the tattoo parlor. Brock's was a falcon which symbolized his spirit guide although it looked suspiciously like certain Air Force emblems and would later make fans of his movies think he had been in the military.

When Brock was seventeen he met the man who would make him a porn star. The man did not know Brock was seventeen at first, but once he discovered this he had Brock move in with him and prepared him to become a porn star after his eighteenth birthday. Brock did not know what happened to his girlfriend. The man was very generous to him but Brock was not fond of him genuinely. The man liked to sodomize him and it always hurt but Brock pretended he liked it.

Brock wanted to be a rock and roll star so the man bought him a black Les Paul electric guitar and an amplifier. He permitted Brock to get his own apartment and to have friends, mostly other hustlers. The man had Brock cut his hair short and for one year, Brock made one or two, and once three, porn movies a month. In general, he would not like the boys or men he had to have sex with but he would often find a friend among the boys he did not have to have sex with. Sometimes he would have real sex with these boys after the movie was done, although the man did not like it when he did. Sometimes he had to go to parties with one of the stuck-up gay faggot boys he did not like and they had to perform with each other while rich men groped them.

By the end of that year, Brock was being put on the cover of porn videotape boxes. He had a made-up name the man had made up. Brock thought it sounded dumb. He had grown to dislike the man even more than he had disliked his parents. He disliked having his hair cut short and blown dry and styled for the movies. Brock had one good friend, another porn star; and these two boys had nonpenetrative sex, and Brock had penetrative sex with his friend's girlfriend as well. His friend knew this and more or less approved.

Brock got to meet some famous men but none of them were interested in who he was or where he came from or the fact he wanted to be a rock and roll star. These men were interested in him sexually, and interested in cocaine. Once Brock and his friend the other porn star stole some money and cocaine from a very rich man. Brock's boss became very angry and told Brock he would have his friend arrested and sent to jail. This made Brock very angry and he beat his boss very severely and ran away. He did not go very far, though, and soon his boss was calling for him to come back because he thought he loved Brock, despite the beating.

Brock came back but then he stabbed his boss eight times

with a fruit knife, almost but not quite killing him. Brock was in jail for a while but he was not indicted for anything so they let him go and he moved to San Francisco with his friend the other porn star. He took his Les Paul guitar with him. He let his hair grow out. He wanted his friend to be his boyfriend but the friend liked girls better and didn't want to have sex with men once he stopped doing porn movies. Instead they shot heroin together and lounged around. This was the first and only kind of penetration in their relationship. Brock advertised in a San Francisco paper that he was a porn star and an escort and made some money that way.

Brock's rock career did not take off. He never found anyone who wanted to be in a band with him, and the guys in the bands he auditioned for—ads he found in the straight newspapers—did not like him because he was strange and too aggressive with stories about his life that disturbed them. He fell asleep with a cigarette in an armchair and set it on fire and his friend, who had a job by then, got angry at him. His friend's name was Stan. That wasn't his old porn name, though. Stan took Brock's guitar and sold it because of money Brock owed him.

Brock was sad thinking he and Stan were losing each other. He met an older gay guy—older than him or Stan, anyhow, a guy close to thirty but nice and cool. This guy would have been a good boyfriend for Brock except he already had one. It was okay with the boyfriend if he had sex with Brock, though. They had a very nice apartment and both of them had jobs. They were clean and they had gone to college but they had also done drugs and liked rock music. The guy was very passionate and tender with Brock's body. His boyfriend was kind and amused by Brock's jokes and stories. They made him feel like he could be a decent person given the chance. Sometimes they would all three have sex. They would only fuck Brock, not let him fuck them. Because he had been a porn star they figured that meant something about why they shouldn't let him stick his dick into them. They wanted him to get tested, but that made Brock feel dirty and doomed so he didn't want to. The boyfriend started to get anxious. Then tense, then nervous. Then bitchy, then mean. He didn't want his boyfriend fucking a junkie ex-porn star who could be carrying God knows what. He did not say this directly to Brock but Brock got the picture.

He had not been staying at Stan's much. Stan's girlfriend did not like Brock. When the two boyfriends expelled Brock for the sake of their relationship he could not go back to Stan's until he got drunk and yelled for Stan, then gave up and sat down on the front stoop and cried and cried until Stan let him in. Stan told Brock that he was his best friend and he loved Brock but that it was hard to think about all the stuff they had once done now that he was older and off drugs and knew he was not gay. Stan told Brock he did not think Brock was really gay either, but just that he had been lost and alone and that world had offered him a place so he took it but was never really gay. Brock said no, that he was gay and had always been gay; that it was okay if Stan wasn't and he understood but that Stan shouldn't tell him what he was or wasn't because he didn't know what was in Brock's head really.

Brock left Stan and San Francisco and moved to New York. He contacted his mother and father when he was there. They were happy he was alive but otherwise disconcerted by his reappearance. He borrowed money from them. He got a job as a foot messenger and then, after he had made enough money to buy a secondhand bike, as a bike messenger. He got a room at a single-room occupancy hotel downtown. Brock was twenty-two years old by then. Nobody ever seemed to recognize him for the porn star he had been when he was eighteen and nineteen. In the single-room occupancy hotel, which was on St. Mark's Place, he met a guy who was a student at the New School for Social Research's jazz program, a guy who was black and played the guitar and saxophone and was from Brooklyn and had dreadlocks and was slightly fatter than lots of guys Brock had slept with.

This may have been because this guy was not all that gay. He liked men but was uncomfortable with the idea of gayness. His name was Rodney. Even though he was uncomfortable with the idea of gayness he had bought and looked at gay porn magazines and he was aware from the first that there was something oddly familiar about Brock's face and tattoo. Brock told him—being as honest as he thought he needed to be—that he had been a prostitute after running away from home as a teenager, but he did not tell him that he had been a porn star who once earned a thousand dollars in one night just for letting an entertainment-industry executive probe his anus with his tongue. Well, the man had paid a thousand dollars, in any case. Brock didn't get much of it.

Brock and Rodney lived across the hall from each other on the third floor of the SRO hotel. They kept both their rooms even when they began sleeping together. Brock loved that Rodney could really make the music he'd always wished he had the talent to make. Rodney loved that Brock was beautiful and strangely familiar, obviously desirable yet dangerous and masculine and uncontrolled. He loved Brock's long, straight blond hair. They had sex a lot.

The one drawback of Rodney is that he also liked heroin, although he did not do it as much as Brock used to. He only snorted it at first, but then he brought home works once and wanted Brock to show him how you shot up. This made Brock angry and he cried and they yelled. Rodney got someone else to show him how you shot up and he overdosed and came very close to dying. Because he hadn't died he thought it was funny and told Brock what had happened. Brock was furious but also scared and he said, "I'll do it with you if you promise you'll only ever do it with me, okay? I know this shit, okay? I can't have you cut out on me." Brock had not shot up in eleven months and underestimated his loss of tolerance and died before Rodney knew what was happening.

But we still have the twenty-six movies he made.

The Mother

My inclination is to rush through this. I'd thought Stewart was appallingly stupid when we'd met the year before; he was dating my friend Daniel who liked him because he always had pot. Stewart told me that Jan Brady had died of a drug overdose, meaning Buffy from *Family Affair*; and that no one knew how they had built the Eiffel Tower, meaning the pyramids, though he staunchly resisted these alternatives. "No, Jan Brady." "No, the Eiffel Tower." But when I ran into him about a year later, I was going to school in the city and I didn't have many friends and he liked me, and he didn't seem so stupid to me anymore. His family was rich and socially well placed, they were in the Social Register when I looked it up at the NYU library, and he knew a whole lot of stuff I didn't, important stuff like what restaurants rich people ate at and where they shopped, what kind of clothes they liked, which items sent secret signals only the rich recognized and how complex these codes were.

It's too sickening to even recount. I thought I loved him but he brought out the latent snob in me. He didn't much like that, but I didn't much like being critiqued for my "middle-class" traits—certain sweaters, and such, that he disapproved of, or my haircut, or accent.

The first story I wrote for my writing workshop the next year was about this relationship, and I can't even look at it now, even less think of recounting it again. Stewart was my first boyfriend, we went out for seven months and broke up, the end. It doesn't really go away that easily, since some of my friends now were friends of his roommate Mickey, since lots and lots of things, since my life traces back to that year in a lot of important ways.

I told Mason I was gay and that I was in love. He said he'd figured I was gay, said Ellen asked him if he thought Stewart was my boyfriend, I talked about him every time I saw them. I said, pissed off, "You always figured I was gay?"

Mason smirked. "Yeah, I mean, from when you were about nine or ten, I guess. It's not like you're Mister Inscrutable. Do you want me to act freaked out instead?"

"No," I said sullenly, sinking down in his living room futon.

"Oh, my God," he yelped, running in a circle. "My brother's a homosexual."

"Knock it off."

"He's gonna start cruising the playgrounds, he's going to be arrested . . ."

"Mason, shut up."

"You know," he said, imitating our mother's infamous tone of empathetic concern, "I just want you to be happy. I just worry about the AIDS."

"Mason," I said, drawing my knee up to my chest, "that's not funny."

"I'm sorry. I'm just being stupid." He sat down next to me, put his arm around my shoulder. "It's cool, it's great, I'm glad you're happy. I'm glad you can tell me something like that. I don't care if you're straight or gay or purple or orange, it doesn't make any difference to me."

I leaned against his arm a little. "Do you think," I asked, "that Mom'll really react like that? I mean, should I tell her? I'd like to."

"God," he said, dropping his arm. "Do yourself a favor, don't tell Mom right now. I mean, whatever. Just I doubt now's a good time."

He meant something, obviously. I thought he would just say what but he waited for me to prompt him with raised eyebrows and an expectant look.

"Well . . ." Mason hedged. "I was on this fucking honesty trip myself a few weeks ago. And I told her something. I should've known better but I did."

I looked him right in the eye; and he flinched, tousling my hair. "What the hell are you using on this anyhow?" he said, wiping his hand on his jeans. "It's like fucking Vaseline. I was wondering how you got it so straight."

"Mason," I said, tentatively touching my own hair. It wasn't so greasy. "What did you tell her?"

"Stupid me." He smiled. "I told her about El's abortion."

It was a stunningly stupid thing to reveal, even I knew that. "Why?" My mouth hung open.

"A bug could fly in," he said. I didn't know what he was talking about. "Close your mouth, asshole, I know it was dumb."

"What did she say?"

"Nothing," he said. "She was letting me have it about school, in her—you know—motherly tone; she didn't understand this, she didn't understand that, yak, yak, yak. And I said, you know, something happened last year which really fucked—I didn't say fucked—fucked me up and I was still dealing with it and school was too much for me at the moment. And she asked what. 'Oh, Mason, it's not drugs, is it? Is it something about your brother?' So I just told her. I told her. And she said . . . 'Oh.' "

"What else?"

"Nothing. Just, 'Oh.' I said I wasn't looking for her approval or disapproval, it was done, it was real, and I was feeling like shit about it. Not in a Catholic way, bad, but just because it sucked, I hated it, I wish none of it had ever happened. And she answered me in monosyllables for the rest of the conversation."

I lit up a smoke and Mason passed me half a dented beer can, cut open, with cigarette butts inside. "That was it?" I asked.

"Well, I went out for a while and when I came home she'd left a message on my machine, how I'd really surprised her at first but she realizes people make mistakes and she loves me and she really likes Ellen and she hopes everything will work out, that if I want to talk more to please call her."

"Well, that's cool," I said feebly.

"Fuck that," Mason said. "I called right back and told her I didn't need her fucking half-assed response, that if she couldn't be there when I needed her it's not my job to turn around and give her a rim job for being an uptight, awful mother. That she can say nothing to me when it matters, and then want to be soothed and complimented for being so understanding! Fuck that, I don't need that!"

"You didn't say that stuff," I said, giggling.

"Hell, I didn't," Mason said, his eyes wide. "I said, why do you think the two of us are up here, three hundred miles away from you? Even your fucking precious baby rents an apartment when he comes home so he won't have to stay with you."

"Mason!" I stood up suddenly. "You prick, don't fucking say that. Don't talk about me to Mom like that, that's none of your fucking business to throw at her. That's really fucked up, man. You fucking call her and tell her you came up with that on your own. That's fucked up, Mason, you're an asshole."

"So why did you," he asked snippily, "get your own apartment down there?"

"Fuck you, Mason, you're a prick. I'm going."

He snorted, lighthearted. "Whatever," he said. "Thanks for telling me you're gay," he said, with a snide game-show-host finger gesture.

I paused at the door for a second. "Fuck you, Mason. You made her cry, didn't you?" He nodded, no trace of guilt. "You are such a dick."

"She's not going to cry," he said with put-on cheerfulness, "when you tell her you're a fag. She'll just say, 'Oh,' and ten minutes later wish you luck and hope you don't get AIDS."

I slammed the door behind me and walked straight to Stewart's building. He wasn't home so I took the subway to Grand Central, caught the next train to Bronxville and found Chase and Shelby. They'd just started going out, but acted, as I'd expect from Chase, like an old married couple. I left a message on Stewart's machine and went with Chase and Shelby to the Tap, the old-person's German restaurant they'd started to frequent in my absence. Then we went to a kind of yuppie sports bar over the hill and had beer and potato skins. I slept on Chase's floor, roused the next day by Stewart, who'd driven up to Bronxville and stayed with his parents to find me. He took me back to their house, Tudor-style like all the Pondfield Road "cottages," a picturesque front of half-timber, patterned brick, and sloping slate roofs masking its enormous three-storied bulk. It was furnished as cleanly and impersonally as a small hotel. The only one home was their housekeeper, who let Stewart kiss her cheek and indifferently prepared us sandwiches. Stewart wasn't racist, he'd said once before, because he loved Maddy more than his own mother, and he used to horse around with her son when they were both little kids.

I took a shower, changed into a pair of khakis, an Armani T-shirt, and a navy blue V-neck cotton sweater with a country-club emblem of an Indian chief's head with the word "Siwanoy" below it, embroidered on the chest. I told Stewart I came out to my brother and he asked how it went. I said fine. He said he'd told his parents once, when he was fifteen, at the dinner table but they'd never mentioned it since. "I guess they know," he remarked, surveying my outfit, entirely from his closet. "Or else they think I just run through best friends."

I played with his dog, a yellow Lab, out in the side yard while Stewart got his clothes out of the dryer. "Maddy says," he reported, " 'You don't live here, you ain't bringing me a barrel of clothes from that college of yours, you gonna do that wash yourself.' " When I'd been playing for a while, dog slobber on the country-club sweater, a big black car turned into the driveway. I inched closer to the house but no one came out to save me. The boatlike Mercedes came to a full stop, its engine humming prettily for a moment. Then it fell silent, its heavy door swung open: a lady stepped out.

It was Jacqueline Onassis, I realized. Was Stewart's mother. The camel overcoat, the shiny leather gloves, the sunglasses, the scarf tied over a helmetlike hairdo. The face was a little different, I'll admit, but otherwise it was Jackie O.

"Oh, hello?" She waved as I stepped forward, speaking in a clipped, nasal voice, polite and impervious. "You must be Stewart's friend. I have some groceries in the trunk if you wouldn't mind helping me with them."

The back of the car had sprung open by itself, it seemed. There was one small bag of groceries, some flowers, and a cardboard case of wine bottles nestled down in there. I figured the box of wine would be the gracious thing to carry for her. I gathered that's what she expected.

"Where are you from?" she asked. I said Baltimore, though I figured she wanted a different explanation than that.

"Stewart's father is from Baltimore," she said. I knew that. There's one financial institution of international note in Baltimore, and it bears Stewart's last name, a fairly common one but

Stewart had told me already. His father had grown up in a town house on Mt. Vernon Place, the fanciest square in town, a cluster of New York–sized urban palaces grouped around the towering Washington Monument. Grown up there, Stewart had said, and at an estate on Long Island, and a house in Eton Square in London; then a British boarding school, then Oxford and Harvard. I assumed his father's accent wasn't much like mine.

Only one mother-suitable story popped into my head to give me conversation to offer. While she opened the front door for me, I told her how Stewart and I had been walking down Mercer Street, near the faculty apartments for NYU, and had seen a fat lady walking a chocolate Lab. Stewart elbowed me, said, "Look, there's a brown Caesar dog"—his yellow Lab's name was Caesar; Caesar was running around between us as I followed her through the foyer—and the lady looked up at us with a broad smile, delighted, and declared, "Yes. Why, yes it is."

Stewart's mother set the flowers down on the kitchen table, took off her driving gloves, undid the scarf knotted under her chin. "That's weird," she said tonelessly. "What do you suppose she meant?"

She ruined the fucking story. She was supposed to laugh, say, "How peculiar," and let it go. As it was, she seemed neither amused nor chagrined. It was extremely disconcerting.

"I don't know," I said, grasping at straws to continue. "Either she misheard us," I sighed, "or she was just pleased by the attention."

Stewart came up the back stairs with a folded pile of laundry, trailing a faint smell that mixed fabric softener and marijuana smoke. "Hello," his mother said, unwrapping the flowers from their plastic and placing them, bunch by bunch, in one of the sinks. "Your friend was just telling me a funny story about the dog. We're having your aunt Wendy and uncle Richard over tonight. If you're going to stay you'll have to get your own dinner."

"That's okay," Stewart said, leaving the laundry on a chair. "We're going back in a little bit. I just have to put this in a bag." Stewart went back downstairs to fetch his laundry sack.

"You'll have to excuse me," Stewart's mother said. "I have to start getting ready for dinner."

She didn't leave the room, though. She just turned her back to me, took a glass vase down off a shelf and began rinsing it with water under the kitchen faucet. Filling it partway and swirling to clean the dust out. Stewart came up with his bag, shoved his folded clothes into it. He kissed his mother on the cheek, told her that Caesar was getting too fat and to tell Maddy good-bye and to stop feeding him so much, grabbed my arm and walked me out to his car.

"My mom really liked you," he said, looking out the back window to keep his distance from his mother's Mercedes.

"You think?" I said. The car bumped over the stone edge of a flower bed.

"Shit," he said, red-eyed. "I hope nobody saw that." The little Honda chugged out onto Pondfield Road. "Definitely. If she hadn't liked you, you'd know it."

Rich people scared the fuck out of me, I decided. At first I thought it was just because I wasn't one of them. Daniel called me from Boston some time after that. He was back living with his dad and stepmom, working at a movie theater with a cute punk boy he wanted to seduce. "God, you met The Mother," he exclaimed. "I'm jealous. I never got to meet The Mother."

Michael Mc:_____
A Case Study

The subject was first encountered on Friday, January 29, 1993, at Crow Bar on East Tenth Street, New York City: "1984" night. I don't go to bars much, as I am bad at cruising and small talk. I don't have sex much and when I do I like it to be with a boy I think is cute. My somewhat atypical judgment of cuteness absolves me from any accusations of snobbery or prejudice. The night in question, I had met my friend Astrid, her stepsister Rachel, and my friend Amy at Vazak's bar on the corner of East-Seventh and Avenue B, and we'd drunk a pitcher of Genessee Cream Ale, plus assorted mugs. This was to get into a pleasantly intoxicated state before facing Crow Bar's overpriced bottled beer.

When we arrived at Crow Bar, the girls were hassled for ID as usual (they do not look underage). It was still early—maybe eleven o'clock—and the bar was pretty empty. We played some pinball and danced sporadically to Blondie, David Bowie, and Public Image Ltd. I noticed a kid standing in a dark corner who seemed to be looking at me, an occurrence rare enough to draw my particular attention. Skinny and tall, he had on a long overcoat and a knit hat. What I could see of his face from between his scraggly dreadlocks looked sort of clean and All-American, almost bland except for his nice lips.

He hardly moved from where he was posed, and being unused to being stared at, I kept my eye on him but didn't approach. Ten or so minutes later, with the boy still checking me out, Amy asked me for a cigarette. I pulled out two and handed her one, putting one in my own mouth, and lit them. The boy approached; his face looked even better out of the shadows, definitely grade-A, and his hair was an appealing shade of light reddish-brown. He asked Amy for a cigarette. When she said, "I don't have any—"he turned and headed for the door at a rapid clip, interrupting the "—but my *friend* here does," I knew she intended to add. Now, pressed and lacking a more reasonable alternative, I yelled, "Hey! I have a cigarette!"

His name was Michael. I told him I lived in the neighborhood and he said that he didn't. He told me he was in art school and I told him I drew cartoons. I had one of my cartoon minibooks in my pocket and I gave him one. He asked me to write my phone number on it. Before I knew it, we were making out, standing in the middle of the dance floor while the deejay played "We Are the World." He kneaded my hardening dick through my jeans while I slid my hand down the back of his pants, hidden from public view by his long coat. I grazed his asshole with the tip of my finger while we tongue-kissed. He said he would call me real soon but he needed to catch the train back to his house. I went to sleep smelling his butt on my finger.

Two weeks later he hadn't called. "This shit happens," I said to myself. And to my friends Astrid and Amy, who were wondering, I said, "Cute boys never call me when they say they will." Once again, I would not be getting laid.

Saturday, February 27, 1993: I had been out drinking with my friend Danny, spending most of the night talking about a mutual friend's problem with heroin. I returned to my home at 700 East Ninth Street and went to bed at approximately 2:21 A.M. I awoke in confusion to a flurry of beeps from my answering machine, and this message: "Hey, this is Mike . . . I met you at Crow Bar. I was wondering . . . what you're doing . . . 'cause I really wanna . . . you know, get together . . . but I guess you're not around . . . I'll call back in a few days." while he spoke, I went nuts trying to figure out what time it was (3:48 A.M.) and where the phone was (living room). By the time I had traced the telephone line from its outlet to the actual set, he had hung up.

And he didn't call back in a few days.

Thursday, March 12, 1993: He finally reached me at home. We made a date for him to come over the next day. I was not confident, at this point, that he would actually show up, but close enough to the appointed time my doorbell rang. By this time I had pretty much forgotten what he looked like. He was taller and skinnier that I'd remembered, with a bigger head. I'd embellished my image of him a sort of a Gothic type, but he was wearing a Timberland jacket, a turtleneck, sweatpants, and those highly padded high-top sneakers with white tube socks. He called me "kid" and said "whassup." We didn't kiss then, and I wasn't sure what the terms of our interaction would be, whether it was to be hot sex or "first-date." I decided to act "first-date," at least for the moment. I suggested we get some movies and some beer. At Kim's Video I picked out Andy Warhol's *Flesh,* because Mike was studying film and he said he'd never seen it. We bought some forty-ouncers, and as we walked back across Tompkins Square Park, I was very satisfied to be seen walking with this kid. I didn't run into anyone I know.

I put in the movie and we started watching. I was on the couch and he sat down on the floor to my left. He sat down and started talking nonstop, about going to film school and his old apartment in the Bronx and how sucky it was to have to live with his parents. He talked about the ins and outs of bicycle messengery. (My friends tell me that I have a tendency to ramble on endlessly about myself; I suppose this was my comeuppance.) Suddenly he shut his mouth and looked at me, and I scooted down on the floor and started kissing him. He was already hard. We got our hands into each other's pants, and I wrapped my fist around his cock and started jerking him off. Kicking off his sneakers, he pulled his pants and underwear entirely off, unzipped my pants, pulled my dick free and started sucking it. His dick was really thick but comparatively short, maybe four inches long, with bristly clipped blond pubes. I hadn't pegged him for a pube clipper. I rubbed beneath his balls, moving towards his asshole, and he arched his back like a cat, keeping my dick in his mouth. He wasn't that good a cocksucker. I said, "Let's go into my room." I was afraid my roommate John, the twenty-three-year-old heterosexual associate editor of a prestigious Marxist monthly, would show up soon.

Once in bed and thoroughly naked, Mike and I sixty-nined for a while, but it was clear that his butt was where it was at: he moaned and squirmed whenever I got near it. While he kept sucking me off, getting better little by little, I poked and licked his butthole, which was smooth and hairless without much pucker around it, just a clean pink hole between his cheeks. It was surprisingly loose too; I could get three fingers in it almost right away, and the more I finger-fucked him, the prettier and puffier his asslips became. Without saying a word, he got on his knees, rubbed his ass in my face, and braced himself against the head of my bed. I picked my recently purchased package of Trojans off the bookshelf by my bed, got one out, opened it and rolled it down my cock, lubing it with spit. I slid it right up his ass, and he pushed back at me, his bony ass pushing against my groin. I ran my hands along his torso, making him grunt appealingly as I pinched his nipples. I could feel his ass twitching as he got ready to shoot his load onto my sheets, and he thrashed wildly as he came. I pulled out then. When I used to get fucked I always thought it hurt to get fucked after I came, so I was trying to be considerate. I hoped he would suck me some more and try to get me off, but instead he started talking again.

He told me that he was a dread—not a Rastafarian, he made

clear, because he was white and thought it was stupid that white American kids thought they could become Rastafarians just by smoking pot, listening to reggae, and growing dreads. But he respected that philosophy, for the most part. There were some things he disagreed with, of course. "Like a lot of Rastafarians think that if a person is gay, what you should do is hit them in the head with a rock. I don't agree with that," he said in an unusual, detached tone. Then he began explaining his theory of sexuality while I lazily jerked off my half-hard cock: "I'm bisexual. I think that when you want to fuck, when you want to do it to somebody, you go with a girl, and when you want to be the one who lets go, who gets done to, you go with a guy." He expressed the desire to dress up in women's clothes "sometime," because sometimes he wanted to be a woman, and get fucked. He was sliding closer to me on the bed, and I was jerking his dick a little too. He pushed against me close and the head of my dick started to feel warm and snug: I realized that the poor, unlatexed thing was nestling just slightly inside his poop shoot. He said that he wanted to feel feminine. I thought about fucking him a little without a rubber, because he wasn't asking. I bent down and sucked on his dick some while thinking about it. Doesn't he notice that I'm up his ass? I wondered. But I put on a condom—hooray for me—before I started drilling him again.

He said, "I've never let anyone do this before. You're the first guy that's ever fucked me." I didn't think he was lying. Some boys just have naturally loose buttholes. He needed five bucks to get to the train station on time.

Saturday, April 17, 1993: Mike called me just after I had announced giving up hope. He was in his bedroom at his parents' house on Long Island, thinking about me (circa 2:10 A.M.). We talked small talk for a while. He asked me why I didn't talk about myself very much. I said I was shy and he said that was no excuse, he was shy too. He told me he had run into a friend who was a girl who he used to go out with and that they had had a fight, which had made him sad. Somehow we got back on the topic of women's clothes. This is what he said he wanted to do:

I was to pick out a dress for him. I thought a snug black dress like my girlfriends wear to go out would be nice (Astrid has a very pretty one by Michael Kors, which she wore when we lurked outside of Café Tabac, looking for Madonna on the night of her birthday party there). But no—Mike wanted a leather miniskirt with fishnets and high heels. He wanted me to take him out dancing to a nice straight nightclub, believing, at a great stretch of the imagination, that he could pass as a real woman if he tried. I would let everyone see that he was my woman, he said. We would make out on the dance floor and he would rub my dick. Then we'd go to a dark corner and I'd slide my hand up into his panties and feel his secret surprise which was just for me. Then I could finger his hole and get him all relaxed and loose. Then I could take my big hard cock and stick it in him, push it in and pull it out, screw his pussy, let him feel it, fuck his pussy so hard, make him come . . .

We came. I shot a load of runny white sperm over my stomach and thigh as I held the phone to my ear, sitting on the edge of my bed. He was panting, with three of his own fingers—if his description can be trusted—firmly shoved up his ass. He asked me, "Can we really do it?" I said sure. He said, "I'll have to shave my legs . . . would you do it for me, baby?" I said sure.

Friday, June 4, 1993: He called me from one of those weird bars on Bleecker Street where straight people who live outside of Manhattan come to drink. His friends were all drunk and heading home. He wanted to see me. I told him to come on over. I was depressed and tired because I hated my latest job, working on a porn magazine production line. Though I had been employed there for five months, I still felt awkward and unliked in a very junior-high-school sort of way. In a last-ditch gesture of camaraderie, I had contributed my own story of the weird bisexual boy I had slept with to my coworkers' makeshift conversation of sexual adventuring, and it did not seem well received. My boss told me that there was no such thing as bisexuality. I did not understand how a workplace devoted to the production of something as scandalous and unrespectable as homosexual pornography could possibly be so uptight and unpleasant.

This time when we got together, I tried to stick it in too soon, and he complained that it hurt. We sucked each other's dicks and masturbated until he was ready for me to try again. I had to lick out his little butthole for a long time before he said it was okay. "You got a jimmy?" he asked. I did ("jimmy" is a word for "condom," prevalent in hip-hop argot).

Again, he needed a token and a few dollars to get home. He left me his beeper number and told me his last name, Carlisle, and his age, eighteen.

Friday, September 17, 1993: I hadn't heard from Mike in several months. I beeped him a bunch of times but never got a call back. I called Information and they had no Michael Carlisles listed in any of the Long Island towns I vaguely remembered him mentioning. Then I gave up.

"I've been in the hospital," he said when he called. "I got run over by a bus and broke my arm." He still had a cast when he came over, and I had to fuck him facedown with his arm hanging off the edge of the bed.

He was tired and wanted to spend the night, but insisted on sleeping on the couch, so I wouldn't bump his arm. When we left the safety of my room, I ran into a girl in the hallway. Apparently my roommate John was getting some that night too. Neither Mike nor I was that naked or anything, but our appearance confounded her: a couple of long-haired tattooed boys in their underpants. I know all this because she's now my friend Sara. I ran into her at a queer film festival a few weeks later and she said, "Hey, remember me? I slept with your roommate!" Sara was a Riot Grrrl at the time.

After we got to be friends, she told me this story: "I asked John who those boys were hanging out in your living room, and he said, 'Oh, that's my roommate and his friend.' I said, 'I thought you said your roommate is gay,' and he said, 'Yeah, he is, that's the guy he has sex with.' I said, 'Wow, I just thought they looked like weird straight boys who'd listen to Pearl Jam or something,' and John said, 'Bard has critical issues with gay culture.' "

———————

Saturday, October 2, 1993: Mike called me at 2:45 A.M. He was at a friend's house "in the city" and wanted to come over, but needed directions. It turned out his friend lived in Far Rockaway, about as far from Manhattan as you can get on the subway. He was sloshed and it took hours for him to come over. He called again at about 5:05 A.M. and said he'd forgotten my address. I looked up from the phone and out the window and saw him talking on the pay phone on the opposite corner.

I sucked his dick, he sucked mine, I rimmed him, we fucked. We were getting into a routine. Afterward he told me a story about his boss at the bicycle messenger service. The guy always talked about porno movies, and Mike said, "he's always talking about how big the guys' dicks were, how great they looked sliding in and out of the girl's pussy or her mouth, always just really obsessed with the guys' dicks. I asked him if he ever watches the movies where two girls do it to each other, and he said, 'No way, man. That shit is a sin. I don't watch that gay shit.' " I liked that story. I felt that it demonstrated an innate intelligence, a sense of irony that had been lacking in his earlier comments about the Rastafarian perspective on homosexuality.

The next morning we sucked each other off and laid around in bed. Suddenly at eleven o'clock he jumped up and asked to use the phone. His friend who'd driven him to Far Rockaway from Long Island had already gone home, and so he called her mother and left a snotty message about how he really appreciated her waiting for him like she said she would.

Not too long after (Tuesday, November 9, 1993), I got fired from my job and had to give up my slick East Village apartment. I moved into the crawl space under the stairs in my friend Amy's apartment. Mike didn't have a beeper anymore, since his accident had forestalled his career in bicycle messengery. I went to Boston, then San Francisco for a while—where, to my chagrin, I found no Cute Boys—and worked my way back East on the trains, visiting Astrid who'd left New York to go to graduate school in Milwaukee, a city bubbling over with weird straight boys who looked like they'd listen to Pearl Jam, and finally back to New York City on Thursday, February 3. Amy told me that Mike had called looking for me. He had tracked me down.

He came over for a slap and tickle. I could not lure him into my cozy cubbyhole, as he claimed to be claustrophobic, so I had to duke him all around the living room. For a while, he was coming over as frequently as every two weeks. He was starting to get on my nerves. I'd discovered that his last name wasn't Carlisle, and when I tried to recall why exactly I thought it was, I couldn't come up with anything (I do know what his last name is now, but since it is actually his last name, I feel it only proper to withhold it). We were always being caught doing it by one or another of the five people who shared the apartment. I was liking fucking him facedown or doggy style just so I could look at my dick sliding in and out of his ass thinking about the boys I really wished I was fucking.

His sexual demands were getting increasingly irritating. He tried on clothes from Amy's closet and made me fuck him with her pantyhose around his knees. He decided he might be into S & M a little and demanded that I tie him up and drip hot wax on his nipples and down his butt crack. Unable to ride his bike or play basketball, he'd put on weight and had developed a little belly. I smacked him around a little after he bugged me to. I got really pissed once when he asked me if I was finished with my beer—there was an inch or so left at the bottom—and I said sure because I thought he wanted to drink the rest. Instead he stuck it up his butt and tried to put on a show. He had gotten a job dancing at Show Palace and done it once, not sure if he wanted to go back or not. He told me about the old guys touching his dick. Some of them had made offers. He asked me if I thought that was dirty. I said I don't know. If you want it to be.

We were doing it on Amy's futon when she came home with some of her friends to watch *Saturday Night Live*. Mike demanded to know who was out there. "See if anybody wants to watch us." Totally whipped at this point, I ventured out into the living room. "Amy," I said, "Mike and I are having sex. You wouldn't want to watch, would you?" She raised her eyebrows, burped, and said, "Why not?"

Mike and I just fucked for a while, but he was intent on pulling her into it. Anyhow, I always had the fantasy of fucking a boy up the ass while he ate out a girl. I think he may have fucked her after I fell asleep. She's said a couple things that sound vague and slightly guilt-ridden. The next morning, our other roommate Ann-Marie opened the door to ask Amy a question and was surprised to find the three of us in bed. Her boyfriend Barney (an exceptionally handsome East Village squatter recently dispossessed from the late lamented Glass House, a renowned squat that had been shut up by the police) soon popped his head in too, made himself at home on the floor, and began talking with Mike about what kinds of guns could pass through metal detectors. Barney expressed interest in getting his hands on a Glock—for self-defense, of course—and Mike told him that he knew how to set him up with one cheap. There was a certain evident kinship between them. It was not reassuring.

The next couple times he came over, I'd only listen to him talk for a few minutes before I'd get him on his stomach and stick it in his can. I thought about other boys I'd like to screw while duking him, and I'd try to get him out of the house as soon as I could. I am not a callous person by any means. It's just how I felt. The novelty had sort of worn off, and was not yet replaced with any other consolatory sentiment.

On Saturday, April 23, 1994, I fucked him on the couch until I came, then slid down onto the floor to suck him off. My couch, incidentally, is wicker—not like the crap you see at Pier One, but heavy and solid and square—and a single futon fits just perfectly into it: this detail figures prominently in a few moments. So I was sucking him off, hoping to make him come so he would put on his clothes and leave. Mike said something like, "I could enjoy you doing that for hours," which indicated to me that he was not concentrating on getting off. I got him to sit up a little so I could jerk him off better, and he looked down at my dick and said, "Whoa, was that like that when we were fucking?"

I looked down at the condom that was still on my dick. At

least the bottom part of it was still around my dick. The torn part of it was hanging off. I said to myself (I think to myself, perhaps I said it out loud), "This must have just broke . . ." And before I could complete my thought, or protest, with the words " 'cause it's still filled with cum," all of the runny, transparent semen dripped to the floor in one runny gob.

I concluded that the condom must have dried out during the twenty minutes I was sucking his dick, caught on the wicker of the couch and torn. Unfortunately, Mike did not see the little pool of stale semen hit the floor. He was upset. He wanted to know if I had any diseases. He said that this was a matter of life and death and called me "bra."

I explained what I thought was my exceptionally likely interpretation of events several times. Then I realized that, despite its logic, it sounded like a fat lie. That made me sound anxious and, therefore, sound like a fat liar. I was not happy.

The easiest thing in the world would have been to say I don't have any diseases, but I couldn't bring myself to do it, despite the fact that I don't have any diseases except occasionally athlete's foot. The right answer to "Do you have any diseases?" is "No. I got tested a few months ago and I'm clean." This would be a lie. I do not have the required certification. I have never been tested for HIV, have had very little in the course of my sexual history to make me think I should. I mean, I've never even had crabs. In my opinion, this is an altogether reasonable outlook. So here I am finally faced with the consequences of my beliefs: I am aware that any sexual act has the potential for putting you at some risk. But this is not a comforting thing to say to someone who thinks a condom just broke in his ass. It sounds like a used-car salesman saying, "Well, you should have checked the carburetor before you paid me three thousand dollars for it."

To put it succinctly, I was fucked. There was nothing I could think of to say that didn't sound like a lie.

I said that I was pretty sure that I was okay, but that this was something we should talk about. That having sex with guys means thinking about stuff like this, and that if he didn't want to think about it, then he shouldn't be doing it.

He agreed that maybe he shouldn't.

I told him that he absolutely must call me in the next week or so and we would talk seriously about it. I said I have never asked you to promise me anything but you must promise to call. He said he would. He didn't.

I guess I had enjoyed the thrill of embodying the strange, mysterious world of queersex. This was its opposite face, and I did not enjoy it. I said to myself, he's the one who used to be heavy into dope, he's the one who fucks strange girls all over town, and maybe a lot more I don't know about. Why do I get to be the wellspring of HIV? When he didn't call me like he promised he would, I decided I wouldn't see him anymore.

He did not call again. However, four months later, on Friday, June 19, 1994, he came by without calling and we had sex, despite the decision I had made. This was about the same time that a song entitled "Self Esteem," by the band Offspring, which dealt with precisely this situation, began being played on the radio a lot. Mike doesn't like that kind of music, however. I filled up my five-disc CD player with all of my hip-hop albums—House of Pain, Gang Starr, Beastie Boys, Digable Planets, Lords of the Underground—not necessarily your hardest collection, but all I had. He didn't mention the ripped-condom incident and neither did I. However, I did make sure to have nice new Ramses on hand, rather than Lifestyles, which I've decided are crappy. When Mike came over, he wasn't drunk at all. Myself, I had gotten a job, and when Amy moved out to go to California for a couple months, I took over the lease and her bedroom. It had been ages since Mike and I had gotten to mess around in my own bed in my own room, and I stripped him of his clothes and we rolled around naked, sucking each other's dicks. At a certain point, he pushed me down on my back and straddled me, holding my dick and guiding it up his ass: he'd never been quite so aggressive in getting fucked before. It sort of hurt. My dick wasn't being rubbed the right way and I kept hitting his pelvic bones at a bad angle, but he was hard as a rock, biting his lip as he slid up and down on my cock. The visuals were great—I've been able to masturbate numerous times remembering his facial expression, the way his stomach looked as he arched his back, the way his small, hard nipples felt between my fingers. I could lick the head of his dick as it poked out at me, and after a few loud groans, he shot a load onto my chest. I moved his ass a little so his weight was resting more on me, and fucked him quick and furious at a more satisfying angle, and came pretty soon after that. I told him that sometime I might like him to fuck me. He said, "I don't know. I've never done that before."

––––––––

I came home from work a few weeks later—Thursday, September 8, 1994—and was surprised to find him sitting on the couch talking to my friend Spot, who I was letting stay with me for complex reasons really beyond the scope of this essay. It was almost still light outside, and I don't think I'd ever seen him so early in the day. He was back in school, and told me about one of his teachers who had it out for him, who believed that he was "always stoned." He said he was trying to get his shit together, was going to quit drinking, quit smoking ("except for herb, which is natural"), and quit cutting classes.

When Spot left, I shut my bedroom door. Mike had on girl's underpants, black satin with lace trim, when I took down his jeans. I accepted this without inquiry. I rubbed his dick through the satin and he took off his shirt: his chest was shaved. He said some guy he met was paying him a hundred dollars to take pictures of him and asked him to shave his chest smooth. As a dread, he felt that cutting hair was wrong, and felt some conflict about having done this. He said he'd never do it again. "I want to make you come," he said. "You never just let me suck your dick until you come." He took off his panties and knelt down between my legs, hauled out my cock and started sucking on it. I held the back of his head by the dreadlocks and fucked his face a little harder than I'd done before. He was really good at sucking dick by this point, and pretty good at sucking my dick in particular. He was jerking off while giving me head. When I was about to come, I said, "I'm going to come," hoping slightly that he wouldn't take his mouth off it. He did, though, and I shot my wad onto his hair, neck, and chest. Then he stood up and put his butt in my face, jerking off while I licked his asshole and balls. I pushed him down on the bed and sucked his dick while moving three fingers around in his ass. He came all over his stomach.

Smoking cigarettes afterward—he had two Newports left in a pack and said he wasn't going to buy any more after this—he told me he wasn't sure how he felt about getting fucked anymore. He was starting to think that sex for the sake of pleasure was wrong. He said he was fucking a lot of girls and felt bad about it; that he shouldn't be fucking with people and not loving them. Sex is for having babies with the person you love, he said, and he didn't want a baby or anything right now. He said he didn't know if the person he would love would be a girl or a guy. He said that just because he had to live in Babylon didn't mean he shouldn't keep the rules he believed in. After school, he wanted to go to Africa: that's what was important to him right now.

He said he hadn't planned this or anything, but he wanted to change his life and live according to what he believed. What we'd had was cool and he really liked me a lot, but we shouldn't have sex anymore. He said he would stay in touch and would peep me later ("peep" is a word from the hip-hop argot, meaning "get in touch with; greet"). He gave me a long tongue kiss at the door.

Afterward I told my roommate Chris that I'd gotten dumped. He said that he doubted it. "He'll be back."

Saturday, October 8, 1994, I was watching a movie that I'd rented from Kim's Video with my friends Jodie and Spot. Chris was getting dressed to go out, and the doorbell rang. Our doorbell rings lots, because poorly raised children and drunks hang out on our stoop. I never put any credence in our doorbell. I said, jokingly, "If that's a cute boy, send him up here for me."

A few moments later, Mike knocked at the apartment door.

He was shitfaced, and flopped down on one end of my bed, pretty much passed out cold. We watched the rest of the movie.

After everybody left, I had a hard time moving him so that I could lay in bed. Finally, I woke him up a little and got him to lay on one side of the bed. I took off his shoes, covered him with a blanket, and went to sleep.

I woke up when he started taking off his jeans. My dick was hard, and he pushed his butt back against it. I slid my hand under his shirt and started feeling his stomach. He pulled down his underpants and I felt his dick. He was hard too. I jerked him off and started rubbing my dick between his butt cheeks. He was really grinding his butt on it, and I stuck one finger up his ass. Then I sat up and put my face near his butt, spit on my fingers and really started poking at his hole. I kept poking until I got three fingers way in it, and just looked at his asshole all stretched out. I kissed his butt. I could feel him squeezing my fingers with his ass and knew he was wide awake. I laid back down and turned him around and started kissing him. "Are you going to let me do it?" I asked.

"Do what?" He smiled faintly. He knew damn well what I meant. I could tell he wanted it, but I wasn't going to allow him to think that I stuck my dick in his ass without permission.

"Can I fuck you?" I asked. He shrugged.

"What do you want to do, then?" I asked. He rolled over and put his arms around me, burying his face in my shoulder.

We fell asleep for a while. When we woke up a little later in the night, I sucked his dick and he came on my face. He turned on his side, facing away from me, and I jerked off, spewing come on his butt. When it was finally morning, he put on his clothes, kissed me and left.

It has been a month and a half since I've seen him, pen to paper, Monday, November, 22, 1994. I say it is done now; Chris says, again, "I doubt it."

Some questions for further study:

1. So what is this boy's deal? Do you think I'm really the only guy he sleeps with?

2. What makes him look me up on particular nights? Does he think about me at other times? If so, what does he think?

3. Did it turn him off when I told him I wanted him to fuck me sometime? Did this disrupt his internal rules for having sex with a guy?

4. Sometimes I think I'm sort of in love with him. I told him that once, that I was sort of in love with him. Do you think he's sort of in love with me?

Additional Selected Lives
in Brief

James Loughlin Childes

James Loughlin Childes was born in Yonkers, New York, the youngest of his parents' five children. Two of his older brothers went to Vietnam and one was killed and one moved to North Carolina and opened a motorcycle shop. This one was his older brother Shawn. Shawn got married and would come and visit his family with his new wife, who was not Catholic. James wanted to go stay with them sometimes but his parents did not encourage him in this, which allowed James to think that Shawn would permit it. Actually he wouldn't have.

It was hard for James to find a job when he graduated high school in 1979. His parents wanted him to go to college but he did not want to. Only his two older sisters had been to college, community college. His dad was an electrician and James became his electrician's helper. He liked to drink beer and watch sports and play darts at a local bar, and he liked to look at motorcycles. His mother worried that he was irresponsible mostly because he did not date any girls seriously. She would not have minded him not going to college and not getting a job on his own if he had shown an inclination to get married and own his own house.

James liked motorcycles at first, and then he also came to like leather jackets and leather chaps and leather hats. He liked leather with metal studs in it. There were bars in the city where men wore such outfits and drank beer and, sometimes, played darts. James liked the older men who drove trucks or had other working-class jobs, and he did not like so much the older men who were doctors or lawyers but dressed up in leather for fun, even if they had very nice motorcycles. Such men did not like him much either because he did not show much need of being shaped or guided and he could not be made more intelligent or sophisticated because he did not value those things. He valued intelligence but did not see it in the same way.

He thought of the men he had sexual relations with as his friends. Often, the things they did together were only by a stretch of the definition sexual. He enjoyed being talked to harshly, being handled roughly, slapped, pinched and poked. It was funny. James always felt as if he were ready to burst into a smile but the men he played with did not smile during these games so James tried to hold back. James felt certain the men knew the games were funny, though. Otherwise they were very nice. One man helped James get a union card so he could do electricians' work for new buildings in the city. Another helped him find a nice rent-controlled apartment in Washington Heights.

Later, in the late mid-eighties, James had an especial friend who was a guidance counselor at a Bronx high school. This friend was intelligent and had many opinions. One was that the gay community should not support the North American Man Boy Love Association. Another was that the gay community did not respect leathermen even though they were among the small group of people that actually made things happen. This friend was a member of a political group of gay Democrats. He was fifteen years older than James and he became sick with AIDS and died. While he was sick James thought of little besides taking care of him, but after he died, James became very angry at the circumstances which had caused his friend's death. He began to have opinions of his own, even though they were guided by what he thought his friend might have told him. He was angry that people said gay people brought AIDS on themselves. He was angry with other gay people for saying that men like his friend did all sorts of nasty things and brought AIDS on themselves. First, it was not true that his friend did nasty things and second he did not believe it was right to say anyone brought AIDS on themselves.

James's parents tried to behave as if his life as a gay leatherman did not bother them, but it did. They wished he would stop but by then there was little else they knew of in his life so it was impossible to imagine what he would be if he was not a gay leatherman. He talked on the phone to his brother Shawn, who had, to a certain degree, become a Southern redneck but who also remained an outlaw biker, and though he discussed issues of sexuality and moral right and wrong in crude terms he was basically a more understanding person than James's parents were.

James would be mad if any gay person in any of the groups he belonged to suggested that James was a bad image for them to represent to society. These people were often but not always male and he did not know what they thought was so much better about themselves. Actually, he did know what they thought was better, but he liked to say he didn't. They thought they were more respectable-looking. They thought they looked less like bad homosexuals. They did not simply think this was better public relations, they believed it truly made them better people.

James did not look all that much like a bad homosexual, as such stereotypes are defined. He only looked like a nasty leather guy to other homosexuals who were uptight about straight people thinking about such things. To straight people James looked like a thirty-year-old biker guy. He didn't wear chaps all over and he didn't parade in a leather thong with his nipple rings showing because, for one, his dead friend had not thought that such spectacles were proper from a political point of view; and for another thing he didn't have those kinds of inclinations towards spectacle anywhere in himself.

The month that James turned thirty, he had a very unfortunate accident on his motorcycle. A car did not stop at a red light and struck him and ran him over. He was not killed because he had seen the car coming and tried to turn away and so it did not hit him full on at his top speed and it did not throw him into the air. The car simply knocked him onto the ground and then rolled over the lower part of his body.

James was in the hospital afterwards for eight months. When he came out he had to use a wheelchair although in therapy he was learning how to walk with braces. He was not very good at using the braces. It was not easy considering his injuries. He had to live with his parents for several months and give up his apartment in Washington Heights.

Eventually, a friend who lived on Lexington Avenue in an elevator building rescued James by renting him one of the rooms cheaply. They had met in a grief group a few years earlier and this friend had lost his lover also. They were very generous to each other but not extraordinarily compatible. They did not understand each other on a deep personal level but being nice helped. James cooked and cleaned a lot for this friend; for his part the friend helped James with his bills and getting around outside.

James found that many of the places he wanted to go as a gay leatherman were difficult to get to in a wheelchair, and even if he could get there it was difficult to be there in a wheelchair. He could get into his favorite bar with some assistance but once there he could not see over the bar, and he could not sit easily with his friends because the bar was small and crowded and the side tables were designed to be stood at. His head was at the level of everyone else's beer gut. This made him very self-conscious. Even when a man looked at him because he had a handsome face and an appealing style, James was convinced he was being stared at because he was in a wheelchair.

Truthfully, his wheelchair did affect the way men looked at him, even if, or especially if, they found him attractive. Because he was so low it was hard to casually start a conversation with him. It was difficult for James to make use of standard ruses to start a conversation too. Someone at eye level always had matches before any man would look down and see James offering a light. His roommate was almost always with him, to help him get around in taxis and on the subway and in and out of bars; because they were always seen together, some men concluded they were boyfriends and that they should leave James alone.

Another barrier was that men did not know what James could do or couldn't do, sexually, with his injuries. They were scared of finding themselves in an unexpected position. They were afraid of whether his penis would work or not, if he would have emotional issues that would frighten them.

Sometimes people thought he was in a wheelchair because of something to do with AIDS, and often these were the nicest gay men he met—they made the effort to go out of their way and offer support—but they seemed taken aback when he explained he had been in a motorcycle accident. They had learned not to see AIDS as something to be guilty about but a motorcycle accident seemed suspicious because James might have been drunk, in which case maybe it was his own fault. Motorcycle accidents were not part of the plague gay people faced generally so they had not learned to contextualize it as a fate.

James began to feel that it was wrong that AIDS was the only disability gay people acknowledged. His friend with the elevator apartment took him to a leatherman social event at the Lesbian and Gay Community Center and he met a leather lesbian in a wheelchair there and she agreed. The leather lesbian's name was Connie, she had a girlfriend, she had multiple sclerosis, and she was a member of a group for gay disableds. She was older than James and very smart. She reminded him of his dead friend because she was smart and political and meant well toward people. Connie was a caseworker who counseled women getting out of prison. She lived in Park Slope in a brownstone that was outfitted very well for people in wheelchairs. There were no apartments available but there was a waiting list and Connie said she would help James get on it. She said he should start coming to the group she was a member of, and James did.

This group talked about personal stuff and they also talked about issues like gay organizations having benefits and socials and meetings in clubs or other facilities that were not really wheelchair accessible. Or sometimes were not equipped for deaf or blind people. You would not believe it, the offenses were often so obvious, not mediated at all by even the slightest pretense for concern. One would have thought it was the people with disabilities themselves who were causing trouble for the gays by their difficult demands to be included. One night James ended up talking to a young man who had cerebral palsy and had always liked motorcycles but had never ridden one. This young man had wanted to wear leather but had never done so. They had coffee after a meeting and James told the young man about driving his motorcycle to North Carolina to visit his brother, and then down to Key West with his brother and his brother's wife on their hogs.

The young man had been protected by his family and they had been upset when he did not move back to Connecticut after finishing his schooling at NYU. Even though he only really walked a little funny they wanted to believe he needed them to take care of him. James thought this young man was much braver than him since he had pursued and won an independence for himself, while James himself had only had to regain an independence he already knew and could not have lived without. This young man thought James was very sexy and James liked him too, although he was ashamed of himself somewhat for evaluating the degree of the young man's disability and being glad it wasn't so severe as to affect his looks. James could not help but consider some disabilities as deformities, at least as far as his personal sexual attractedness went.

James's doctor told him that he might be able to walk with braces better if they amputated his left leg below the knee and put in some metal to re-create his hip socket. James did not feel good about this decision at first because he had been somewhat relieved that his lower body looked normal even if it didn't work normal. He was not comfortable with cutting off a part of his body that he could see and feel and touch. All he could picture was his leg on a tray, no longer a part of him. A little death. Connie told him that he should think about it; it was an opportunity, it did not sound great right off the bat, certainly, but it would do things for him; things she would want if she had the opportunity to have them. Connie said all she could expect was to become less mobile as time went on, but James did not have a disease, he had an injury, and he should seriously consider whatever options helped him to compensate for that injury.

The young man, who was by now James's lover, held him while he thought about it, pressing their bodies close together. James decided being able to walk somewhat would be better than the chair. He was still not good with the chair but he had often broken things in his youth and had often walked on crutches. If he could put weight on his hip and put weight on an artificial leg, he could certainly use the braces then. He thought he might want a shiny black artificial leg since the flesh-tone ones they showed him did not look very lifelike anyway. This proved to be too expensive, though, and would not be covered by Medicaid.

The hospital incinerated James's amputated leg although he had expressed a desire to look at it. They had not taken his request seriously. James was somewhat annoyed and somewhat relieved—annoyed not to have been listened to, relieved not to have seen it. The young man was glad to have James home afterward and kissed him and leaned across his lap and pulled his T-shirt over his head and undid James's button-up plaid flannel shirt. He peeked under the bandages on James's hip and traced the metal armature that penetrated James's firm white flesh in several places. He said, "This is the ultimate in piercing, right into the flesh and bone," and, a few kisses later, "You're a cyborg now aren't you? Half man and half metal." James wondered if it would feel any different to make love with one leg. And he found out after a comparatively short wait.

Royl "Lucky" Conors (& Richard Sparks)

Royl Conors was called Lucky because he had been shot in the stomach and arm when he was seventeen. His best friend, Lonnie Sims, was shot in the head and died. Hence, Royl was Lucky, according to the guys in the neighborhood.

Everyone assumed the shooter was someone the boys had known and had angered in their regular routine of petty criminality. That's what Lucky's mother and father and Lonnie's mother and father assumed. They did not believe Lucky when he said he did not know the man. This incident occurred in Dorchester, Massachusetts, in the summer of 1970. The man who shot the boys was never caught and therefore no one ever knew that he shot at the boys because he was angered at the sight of a white boy and a black boy standing around together in what he considered a white neighborhood.

Royl and Lonnie were bad kids, though. It wasn't like Royl was good just because he was not racist enough not to have black friends. He liked to steal and rob and prostitute himself and smoke reefer, and for whatever reason he was sexually attracted to black guys. He and Lonnie used to screw around. Lonnie used to fuck him in the ass and Lonnie's friends fucked him in the ass too, and Royl loved it. He was the only white boy hanging with a group of bad black boys and they fucked him and made fun of him but they actually liked him a lot and no one else could call him the names they called him. If anyone tried they'd get beaten up.

Lonnie had a neighbor who was a college student, a slightly older black guy from New Jersey who lived with his aunt and

uncle while attending Emerson College in Boston. The neighborhood boys were not sure how much they liked him—he was clearly not of their world—but sometimes they would hang out with him because he would buy them beer and smoke reefer with them. His name was Richard Sparks. He was very smart and much more educated than anyone Royl knew. Royl was somewhat offended when Richard wondered why any black people in Boston supported school integration since it was the one city in America where the racists were unquestionably poorer, stupider, and more desperate than the black people; where there was no advantage in putting up with them because their schools were terrible. Richard said property values went up in the poor white neighborhoods when blacks moved in. This was precisely Royl's milieu that Richard was slamming, and though he was offended he could not think of any response that was not simply racist. Which would have made Richard right and his friends angry, so he just shut up and remembered to make fun of Richard, showing up his educated uptightness when he got a chance.

Lonnie told Royl that Richard was queer, that he had queer college friends; that he had gotten Richard to give him money and reefer for fooling around with him. Royl was jealous and mad and irritated by this, and contemptuous of Richard for being a queer, whereas Royl got fucked but was a real male despite this because he was always in control and only wanted it from real hard guys and never begged anyone to do it to him. The guys who fucked him were his friends and they were helping each other out that way.

But then Lonnie got shot and died and Royl became Lucky because he hadn't died. Lucky tried to settle down. Lucky got a girlfriend and got her pregnant, got a job and tried to support her, even though she preferred to live with her parents. Lucky lived with his parents too. His life sucked—he would say. He did not love his girlfriend and his ass ached from not getting fucked. His girlfriend called him a loser because he could not support her. She must have sensed he did not love her. Her mother and Lucky's mother also called him a loser, a bum. But he loved his son. He loved to play with and hold his son, feed him and change his diapers.

One day Lucky ran into Richard on the street and had to tell what had happened to Lonnie. But Richard already knew. Richard wanted to blame Lucky for it but he could not. He had a hard time not regarding Lucky sociologically, as a product of poverty and social stagnation. The other thing he could look at, instead, was Lucky's vital and unconscious sexual aura. Lucky did not hit on Richard. He only permitted his natural effusion, his amiable good will and cluelessness, to settle over Richard like a thin coating of sweat. Richard took him home and gave him beer and made love to him. Lucky knew at once he liked lying underneath Richard much more than trying to be a responsible father in a world of inescapable poverty. But he could not decide any course of action right then.

Neither could Richard. Richard was not yet willing to give up the ideals he had had of love and figure out what to make, really, of his wanting to be with someone like Lucky. His friends certainly did not approve. Richard socialized with other educated and serious-minded black people. Though he did volunteer work for an educational outreach program for city youth and regarded these kids warmly despite the real effects of their disadvantaged background, it seemed different somehow to have a friendship with a poor ignorant white boy—one with the typical arrogance and apparent self-assuredness of a young male surviving a deadly city neighborhood. Richard had friends who were good-looking, well-dressed, socially aware gay black men and some of them had lovers much like themselves and this is what Richard imagined finding one day. Not a white boy with greased hair and a gold chain showing behind the top four unbuttoned buttons of a Red Sox uniform shirt.

Lucky had wanted to name his son Marlon after his dead friend Lonnie but his girlfriend did not. She named the child Tommy and gave it her own last name. Lucky came over to Richard's apartment every other weekend or so and they drank and smoked and made love all evening and when they were done, they would talk about their relationship. Richard would tell Lucky what a beautiful ass he had, how he had fucked a few scrawny bony-assed white boys in his college days and never knew there were white boys with thick, luscious, fleshy bodies like Lucky's. Lucky would say he was afraid he would never see his son again if anyone knew. In Lucky's embrace Richard could cast off his unpleasant brooding about life's problems, his uncertainty about his career, wondering if he'd pleased or disappointed his parents, wondering if his boss thought he was intelligent enough or respected his opinion: their pleasure in each other's bodies seemed to be enough. For Lucky the situation was reversed: Richard talked and thought when the people Lucky knew would have acted or reacted without talking or thinking; Richard mulled over possibilities, considered the unlikely, dreamed about the future.

At the time, Richard did not dare to dream as far as this: that in six or eight years, their interactions as affectionate strangers stealing moments of sexual pleasure together would be only the basis, the history, of a real adult love. That he would drive home from his job as a junior high school teacher, park his car in a driveway, and walk into a kitchen that smelled of pot roast and cabbage and find Lucky in front of the sink peeling carrots in his blue jeans, smiling. That he would be buying science fiction novels to encourage the curiosity of an awkwardly growing eleven-year-old white child who would throw his arms around Richard's neck when he was excited or scared.

Richard did not dare to dream this: he'd be forty-eight years old, a generally happy man who had accomplished some of what he had hoped for in his life while failing at or abandoning some other ambitions; that at nights he would turn, almost in sleep, to the forty-six-year old grandfather next to him, kiss him awake, make love to him. That he would call his lover by his given name, Royl, to see in response a shocked grin. "Nobody's called me that for years," Lucky would say. "That's your name, honey," Richard would say. "No, no it's not," his lover would say, "It's Lucky. You know that."

Richard did not dare to dream like this when he was twenty-three. Instead he gently ran his finger along the curve of a sleeping young man's spine and wondered what would happen to the young man once he'd outgrown this infatuation.

Michael Wheeler

Michael Wheeler's father and mother were divorced when he was a young teenager. This was in the early forties when such things were still relatively uncommon. In fact, they had not discussed the matter beforehand, at least not in Michael's presence, but one day Michael came home from school to find his mother chain-smoking at the breakfast table. She said, "Looks like your father's gone." Michael stood and stared while she stubbed out her cigarette and lit another one. "What are you looking at?" she demanded dismissively. "Ain't nothing I can do about it."

Michael's mother was from Charleston and his father was from Columbia. They lived outside of Columbia. Michael's father used to yell about guessing he didn't make enough money for Michael's mother—that he was not enough of a man for her; that she should have stuck with the boys she met at her horse riding lessons and her debutante parties. Michael's mother would yell, "Why do you have to use my life against me?"

Michael was shy and physically uncoordinated. The neighborhood children had him pegged as a sissy from early on. He liked music class. He wanted to be a music teacher when he grew up and that's what he did become.

Michael married a girl he went to college with, although he suspected even at the time that this was not a wise move. She wanted to have babies but Michael was reluctant.

They moved to a small town in western South Carolina where Michael got a job at the elementary school. After eight years of an unfruitful marriage his wife left him and went back to Greensboro where her family was from.

Michael socialized primarily with other unmarried teachers. His older students, in the fifth or sixth grade, had him pegged as a sissy. They called him "Mr. Squealer." He led the school chorus and directed their plays. There was never any danger of Michael behaving in a sexually inappropriate way with any students, so even though the administrators had him pegged as a sissy they did not worry too much about him. To them, he was in the same category of person as Miss Draylor, the homely unmarried school librarian whom all the adults suspected of an unfulfilled lesbianism: asexual and not worthy of too much serious consideration.

In fact, Michael and Miss Draylor—Susan Draylor—were close friends, and Susan was a lesbian. She was not unfulfilled. Her lover was Mimi Ensor, the proprietress of a flower shop of many years' standing in the town. They often had Michael over for drinks, cards, or supper. They would sing show tunes while Michael played their upright piano. Michael would sing "(I'm Just A Girl Who) Cain't Say No," from the musical *Oklahoma,* or "Cockeyed Optimist" from *South Pacific,* or, later, "I'm Still Here," from Steven Sondheim's *Company.* The women would sing love duets together. Sometimes Mimi would take a notion about a new young man working at her store and invite him to join them. When they were all still relatively young, these fix-ups did not work because very young men found Michael too effeminate and flamboyant, although in the grand scheme of things he really was not so—he had a natural speaking voice that was not deep and manly but the gestures he affected while singing, one of Susan's scarves tied round his neck, were purely invented and ended with the music; and then at a certain point in the passing of years the young men began to be individuals whom Michael remembered from his elementary school choruses. Which placed a different sort of psychological impediment in the way.

But Michael did not mind meeting them again, after losing them, sending them away to high school six or eight or a dozen years before. Once, a young man named Matthew Pease, who was working at Mimi's shop after graduating high school, was brought to dinner. Michael remembered him well, a pretty, overweight boy with pale skin and a soft demeanor that got him pegged as a sissy from early on; a boy with a dramatic, controlled, delicate singing voice. By this point Michael was old, wrinkled, and fat and there was no imagining that Mimi's young men could be lovers for him. No one would have thought of it. Mimi no longer thought of it when she asked them. These evenings were pure amusement, a brief interlude of freedom for three older people whose lives had been painfully circumspect. Matthew sang "Hard-Knock Life" from *Annie,* at the upright piano, affecting sassy, girlish, orphanish gestures. He told the adults that he had considered joining the military, it seemed like the only way he could get the money to go to college. To go to New York, where he wanted to be an actor and Broadway star.

But he was frightened. The Army was a frightening prospect. It might not be so bad, Matthew said, to just stay put at the flower shop.

"Oh, no," Michael said, pausing in his singing of "Sixteen

Going on Seventeen," which he performed with one of Susan's doilies resting on his dyed chestnut pompadour. "If you could take eighteen years of being a faggot in C—— County, you can take four years in the Army. If I was a girl your age again, I'd do it in a heartbeat."

Foo Dog

"When we heard the shotgun blasts—four of them—" Daniel said, "we thought her old boyfriend had come back and killed her. They were always fighting. She told us one day at the mailboxes that she'd broken up with him, he was a creep. Now she was on Prozac, felt better. So we assumed it was this guy, come back to kill her."

"Uh-huh," I said, taking a sip of my beer, Anchor Steam beer. This was a sort-of biker bar, off Haight Street. Not Hell's Angels, nothing all that rough, just a lot of big guys with long hair and leather jackets. I find San Francisco jarring to my personal aesthetics; the city is beautiful but I don't understand the semiotics of the people's wardrobes. I'd asked Daniel if he knew a place where straight and gay people both hung out and he'd folded his eyebrows thinking, not quite understanding my taste but willing to satisfy it, in the same way he might satisfy another visiting friend who wanted to go someplace with young Asian drag queens or cigar-smoking leathermen. In New York it's pretty normal for straight people and gay people to go to the same bar, I think, but maybe that's just me. Or maybe it's just I know people who take drinking more seriously than sex.

"Turns out she had shot herself," Daniel continued with a smile of morbid glee. "But first she had shot each of her three cats."

"She shot her cats?" I repeated with some amount of incredulity.

"Yeah. She really loved them and she was afraid of what would happen to them when she died. That's what someone told me the note said, anyhow."

"You're lucky the pellets didn't come through the ceiling."

"They went through the floor below, I think. It was in the middle of the day, though; the guy in that apartment was at work. I was in the kitchen. Mikey had just been to the store to get cigarettes and heard it from the street." Mikey was Daniel's boyfriend. We'd met him out one night when Daniel was living in New York. "He was coming up the stairs when these cops in body armor threw him against the wall and frisked him. He had to stand against the wall until they'd cleared the apartment. He looked in the door but said you couldn't really see anything—it was one of the cops that told him she'd shot herself."

"There's a movie," I said, "where a lady hangs herself and hangs her cat. Not in the movie, it's about these sisters and their mother killed herself that way. You see Sissy Spacek flipping through a scrapbook and there's this news clipping of a photograph of a woman-shaped body under a sheet and a little sheet with a cat-shaped body under it."

"I don't know if I saw that," Daniel said.

"Anyhow," I said. "It's too bad Mikey didn't do that." Daniel and Mikey had two dogs—Pomeranians—two cats, a parakeet, and an iguana. "By the time the third or fourth pet came sailing past someone's window, someone would have noticed him up there."

Daniel giggled. "Yeah." He sipped his beer and for a second his eyes narrowed to points and he snorted a breath through his nostrils. "He did pick up the dogs. He stormed down the hall and paused, for a second, in the kitchen. And picked up the dogs and kissed them."

"Uh," I said, which was just a sympathetic noise I can make.

"I didn't know what the fuck he was doing."

"How could you know?"

"And then Jane from next door banged on my door and was like, Daniel, I think Mikey's up on the roof. And we ran up the back stairs and when we got up to the roof he wasn't there." His jaw was clenched.

"You don't have to nurse that," I said. "I'm buying tonight."

"Well, if you ever have a boyfriend splats himself off the roof, I guess it'll be my turn," Daniel said, smiling again. "You know, he was wearing my fucking favorite tennis shoes when he did it."

"He didn't mean that, I'm sure."

"He meant it, all right. I saw him put them on. There's no uncertainty about it, this was a big fuck-you to me. I mean: on my fucking birthday."

They had been talking about breaking up for six months or

so. Mikey had been on methadone for as long as I'd known him, hated the program, wanted off it, would end up scoring dope after he skipped his appointment determined to get off the stuff. And he drank a lot and accused Daniel of messing around with other guys and accused me of tolerating him because he was Daniel's boyfriend. Both accusations were occasionally true, but Daniel was a slut when he met him, and I always give off the feeling of tolerating people.

"Things hadn't really been good," Daniel said, "since he set the bed on fire. I was pissed off, obviously. Jane was pretty pissed too, she called me at work and she wasn't so calm about it, a woman with a baby's not really very tolerant of a nodding-out junkie setting the neighboring apartment on fire with his fucking cigarette. I came home and our sheets and pillows and mattress were all on the fucking sidewalk beneath our window, soaking wet. I thought we were going to be evicted."

Daniel and I met Mikey one weekend, probably the first month Daniel moved to New York. He was a go-go dancer we saw at a bar. We both started talking to him and when Daniel goes to the bathroom, Mikey stoops down to say to me, "So, why doesn't your cute friend have a boyfriend?"—which made me too furious for words. I finished my beer and went home and a week later, over at his place, Daniel showed me the little contract the two of them drew up, a covenant of love until death, which they had signed in blood.

They really did this too. It's so fucking queer I wouldn't make it up if it hadn't happened. Michael McInerney—you can look it up on the Internet, the Social Security Death Index. May 17, 1997. Not that his being real necessarily proves the contract existed, but trust me, it's not writerly bullshit.

"Remember in college," I said, "when we fooled around?"

"Yes," Daniel said. Daniel was the first gay guy I was ever friends with. I used to smoke pot with his roommate Jack. Somewhat upset, Jack told me that his roommate was gay. After that, I made a point to befriend him.

"That was lame, wasn't it?" When I came out, I hit on him, because he was the only gay guy I was friends with; and he slept with me, I guess, because he slept with a lot of people. I didn't know it at age nineteen but it was really bad sex.

"Yeah," he said. "It was pretty lame."

"You know, he really loved you a lot."

Daniel shrugged.

"I think he figured if he couldn't make things right with you, he could never make things right ever." Mikey had a fucked-up background, abused kid, teen runaway, teen prostitute and junkie. I felt like I could guess what he felt because I'd thought about killing myself before. It's never because of some awful event. If you're generally a sad person but some one thing has made you happy for a while, it really sucks to lose that one thing. More than if you'd never been happy.

Daniel gulped the last of his beer.

"Mikey can fuck himself. I prayed that he'd come back as a ghost to haunt me so I could tell him to fuck himself every day for the rest of my life."

"I'm just saying—well, in one way I'm just impressed he made it twenty-seven years before doing it," I said.

"I know," Daniel said. "I'll be sad about it one day. Right now I'm still fucking pissed off."

"Another round?" I picked up both glasses with one hand, my thumb in one and my forefinger in the other. I had to squeeze onto one end of the bar and wait for the bartender to notice me. I ordered two Anchor Steams and, when I noticed a small cigarette dispenser behind the counter, a pack of Marlboro reds, which I put in my pocket since I needed both hands to carry the full glasses back to the table.

I set one in front of Daniel and one in front of my place, sat down, and with a flourish produced the fresh pack of cigarettes.

"You know," Daniel said. "I need to get a new pair of tennis shoes tomorrow. Let's go down to the Castro for brunch. San Francisco—even the medics on the ambulance were gay."

"That's probably something to be thankful for," I said, picturing people in emergency uniforms with latex gloves and face masks, contamination suits. I took a big gulp of beer. No one in this bar was really cute. My personal aesthetics were not well satisfied in California. I thought if I disliked the gay guys, the straight guys might be worth looking at, but they weren't. The only cute boy I saw the whole time was panhandling in front of a Walgreen's.

"They cut off his sneakers," Daniel said. "My sneakers, actually. The medic said, 'Maybe you want these?,' and handed me a plastic bag containing these sneakers, splattered with Mikey's blood. You could see it wet on the inside of the bag."

"Ugh," I said.

"Luckily, Jane was at my elbow—'Do you want me to get rid of these for you?' 'Yes, please.'"

We drank for a long time more, and when we got back to his apartment building, Daniel asked me if I wanted to see where Mikey landed. I said no.

The next day we had brunch at Orphan Andy's and Daniel got a pair of tennis shoes at a place on Castro Street. We went shopping downtown and I had the idea to make a movie where we hired a cute gutterpunk like the one I saw in front of Walgreen's to come shopping with us and we'd get him a makeover and dress him up like a female executive, Shisheido makeup and a Donna Karan suit. The last shot of this movie would be him walking down Market Street in his new getup, stumbling in his heels.

I don't know why I found this amusing.

We didn't do it. We did go to the Hoolihan's near Fisherman's Wharf and have strawberry daiquiris, and afterward I made Daniel show me that "krazy loop-de-loop street," which is what I loudly called Lombard Street, hoping to annoy some local tourist-hater. I made Daniel my patented fruit salad and we had some cappuccinos, had lunch, and shopped. We went to an antique store on Market Street and Daniel wanted a sculpture of a monkey and also a little trunk carved with skulls and bones; I knew he wanted both but he kept hedging, so I found something more expensive than the two things put together and bought it for myself. Daniel bought the monkey and the trunk and was happy. He collected monkeys. We admired our purchases, went out to dinner, drank some more, came back, made me a reservation on the airport shuttle, and went to bed. I decided Mikey was an idiot for jumping off such a short building; he could have been crippled for life instead of dead and that would have really ruined everyone's life forever. The next morning I went home, carrying a thirty-five-pound ceramic foo dog wrapped in bubble paper in a shopping bag strategically slit and taped. This was the only way I could carry it, but it looked very much like what they call a "suspicious-looking package."

I was worried that the X-ray machines would show a big foo-dog-shaped black thing and the security would freak out thinking it was filled with Chinese opium resin but they didn't. They just ran it through the machine and didn't say anything. I got home to New York at about four o'clock Sunday afternoon.

Young Hemingways

Since Dale's been on dope, all the stupid, sluggish parts of his personality have become dominant. No joke, man. I was the one who was supposed to be stupid in college. Probably some sort of self-esteem problem in retrospect, but I looked up to him. "It's hard, Jon," he tells me, sunk into a rust-brown armchair by the window of his one-room apartment off Avenue C. "The world can't deal with men anymore. What they call arrogance now they used to call character. They call it sexism now. Yeah." Well, he's always said things like this but he used to be able to dust his pronouncements with quotes from Nietzsche and Herman Melville. Nowadays he sits around with his eyelids drooping shut and can't remember half the books he's read. He's sold most of them, actually, spread out on a blanket off St. Mark's Place. The East Village is one shithole I can't stand. I didn't like it when we shared a sublet the summer between our junior and senior years. I didn't like it when Dale used to drag me down on weekends to drink beer in dumps he said reminded him of Charles Bukowski: the International Bar on First Avenue, where a gin-blossomed old woman in an airy white polyester blouse that showed off her crepe-paper skin turned to me one afternoon and croaked cheerfully, "Wine makes blood." Or Mona's on Avenue B, where groups of dirty new tribalists with rings through their noses shoot hostile looks over at the group of clean-cut kids with their pressed jeans, suspenders, Doc Martens, and swastika tattoos, while Dale relaxes, oblivious, in between. When shadowy men walking to the side of the street hissed, "sess . . . sess . . . sess," I'd cringe, looking dead ahead, in moral not physical terror, living for that big green campus with gates and doors with computer locks and my own mattress on my own dorm floor. I smoke pot, I've tripped out. I'm not some candy-ass. I just hate the smell of desperation. Dale's apartment today, its window open wide, smells just the same as the streets, hopeless. His eyes focus out there, not on me.

It was Dale who said to me, "You should write poetry." Freshman year, sitting at the corner table by the coffee stand, I was telling the story about breaking up with my high school girlfriend a few weeks earlier—a fight about whether or not we'd still be going steady if I wanted to see other people when I was at college. I called her a cunt. Dale asked, seriously, if I'd read much Henry Miller.

A few weeks later, I could say that I had. I read all the books that Dale had loaned me with a fierce hunger, a profound satisfaction in discovering pleasure in words that were rough, ugly, and evocative, like painting the Sistine Chapel in tones mixed from vomit. I despised my parents and high school teachers for having concealed from me the awesome backlist of Grove Press—de Sade to Acker and all the old straight drunks in between. We became visceral artists, rough young intellectuals stranded among the politically correct mob at a former girls' college.

I was just a normal kid—at least that's how I saw myself: a public school dumbshit from a nice but average suburb of Washington, going to college 'cause that's what you did to get a good job after. But I met rich kids at school, people who could afford to worry about what they'd achieve in their lives, not just how they'd survive it. Dale's dad was some hotshit Texas businessman, our friend Foster Smith came from Los Angeles with a Hollywood approach to re-creating Eastern Waspishness, and the one girl we hung out with—considered an equal almost—Tracey Sperber, well, she was already a published author, if you could call it that: her lesbo-feminist mom had collected things she'd said over the first three years of her life and published it as an illustrated volume of poetry entitled *Front Heinies*.

These were my friends. We were all stuck on campus over Thanksgiving break. I couldn't afford to go home so close to Christmas, for which I had bought an expensive airplane ticket, and everyone else loathed their families, or at least pretended to. Me, I was running around, intoxicated in many senses, rolling on empty expanses of lawn, leaves the color of paper bags heaped in magnificent piles in front of complex, empty half-timbered dormitories; yelling and running through the halls of these great, glorified steakhouses built for the daughters of New York's elite, built for people not very much like me but for a weekend mine alone. I climbed through the attic of Dudley Lawrence and, thrusting aside the heavy trap-door, pulled myself onto its roof. Breathing deeply in the cool air, keeping my feet clear of the unguarded edge, I looked off into a horizon of treetops, broken by Tudor chimneys, apartment buildings, a narrow swath of highway: mine.

Later a few of us tough guys got together for dinner at the Argonaut Diner in Yonkers, the shopping-strip suburbia which surrounded us on the blind side, back side of campus. Then we drove in Dale's station wagon to the Eastchester Liquor Express Mart and picked up a couple cases of beer, liberated the Andrews House classroom for our society's inaugural meeting by cracking one small pane of glass and turning the door handle inside. We took turns drinking and reading, drunk, from our journals. It was like *Mr. Chips* or *Dead Poet's Society,* the romantic ideal of education: I was sitting in a classroom with a fireplace and mullioned or munioned or whatevered windows, talking about writing with drunk rich kids.

"Fuckin' brilliant," Foster slurred, dribbling beer down the front of the blue blazer he always wore, his face practically on the table as Tracey dropped her notebook to the floor and stared at it, shocked beyond reasonableness. "The new Mary McCarthy." (McCarthy once taught at our school, actually: she found the students poor and quit after one semester—that was forty years ago, not like I remember her or anything. Nowadays the famous writing professors cash their emeritus paychecks and teach elsewhere.)

Tracey grinned, belched, and grabbed her bottle. "To the new Norman Mailer." And with a nod over in Dale's and my direction, she added, "And the young Hemingways."

This became our monthly ritual, the four of us plus assorted extras, their names changing time from time. The last person standing at our monthly session got named official judge. My poetry sucked, but lots of times I won anyhow. I'd sit alone in my room, looking at the two good lines I'd written, almost shaking; then stick the paper at the very bottom of my desk drawer and knock off something about my girlfriend giving me a handjob. Haikus like "My hand squeezed your tit / Underneath a sac of fat / hard muscles working." Tracey turned away immediately, began scribbling in her notebook. "What are you doing?" I asked. "Writing a haiku about some asshole who gets nailed in the balls by a girl in boots," she said demurely, flicking the ash of her Lucky Strike onto the carpet: Anne Sexton as played by Drew Barrymore. I wanted to fuck her sometimes. I wanted them all to think I was great. I didn't mind if people thought I was sick, or offensive, as long as they thought I had the power to make them feel what I wanted them to.

It's the poetry that matters to me now. Nobody's impressed with that tough-guy shit in the real world, especially when there are twelve-year-olds on the street who'll blow your head off without batting an eye. Man, when I lived in Brooklyn I got mugged by a pair of kids maybe thirteen and ten. The little one had the gun too. He could've shot me dead without risking more than a spanking if he got caught—which he never was. Attitude doesn't count for shit in that situation. Doesn't help you get jobs either. The whole thing's something a college-educated middle-class white boy who writes poetry just better give up at a certain point. Tracey got a fellowship to Iowa and Foster's back in Los Angeles, working in public relations and writing sitcom scripts on spec, cartoons for Nickelodeon. I'm in grad school. Because once Dale said to me, scanning the black-speckled notebook I'd accidentally left in the bathroom we shared, that I should go to grad school. "This is not the bullshit you read us, man. You're ashamed of something inside of you. You're ashamed of what's real in you," he told me, standing in my bathroom door in his boxer shorts as I lay face-down on my bed, pretending to ignore him. "You can jack off for us," he said, "but the Artist tells the truth to himself."

I always sort of knew better anyhow. Nobody who's into frat houses and keg parties and football and date rape ends up studying creative writing at a fartsy liberal arts college, despite the neat ratio of one heterosexual guy per twelve women. The guys at this school—I guess not all—most were retards and spazzes and sissies in their grade schools, their junior highs, maybe all the way down the line. Hell, all my friends in high school were girls too. I don't have any brothers or anything, so the male thing was something I wanted to do for a while.

It's a good idea too. Men are weird. In college you can actually get close to other guys in ways you'll never be able to again: waking, eating, sleeping, all together. Unless I get drafted in the next world war, I won't ever sleep within arm's reach of a male body again. On the other hand, it's only been women I've ever been able to talk to, really, about important stuff. Like this dream I had when I was sixteen, about my uncle, after he'd been dead about six months; too upsetting and way too predictable to bother relating now—you know, grue-some dead stuff, human dread being as trite as it is. When I was nineteen or so I finally got it out to my friend Brooke, my ex-girlfriend from home. Then the next summer, when Dale and I were living together in a sublet on Essex Street below Houston, I tried to tell him about it too, figured I'd go two for two, wanted to place this confidence somewhere within my life, with someone who mattered now, someone I couldn't hide from. I couldn't get the words out. I got agitated and stuttery, sat down on the windowsill, leaning out over the fire escape and seeing trash, graffiti, a man sleeping on cardboard, a clear plastic bag bloated with two-liter bottles beside him. And then Dale said, swallowing, turning on his futon to face the wall, "You don't need to feel pressured to tell me." Don't tell me shit like that, he might as well have said. I don't want to know what goes on inside of you.

He was my only friend right then, besides a few acquaintances also staying in town. I'd gotten a job at Pearl Paint, making less than a hundred fifty dollars a week, borrowing money from my folks to pay for this experiment in independent living. We'd sit up and talk, every night, Dale and me, way too late to make it to work on time, eating peanuts from the bodega downstairs and sipping forty-ouncers of malt liquor, or sometimes Cafe Bustelo, cooked up in an aluminum saucepan. Dale would spin stories, tell me about the Russians he was starting to like, books he read during the day when I was at work. This impressed me, not by the book learning so much as by Dale's passion, his ability to relive these experiences, to put himself in it. In return I offered my stories of skateboarding in construction lots, of running through D.C. streets pursued by mean skinheads who wanted to kick my ass for being a suburban punk.

We didn't go out so much. We had no spare money, just five or ten dollars a day to buy us cigarettes and some dried beans to soak and beer and a paper bag full of nickel candies—Americans have to buy things, we decided, it's our nature, addicted to our regular commodity fix. This is what we discussed. We never managed to talk about feelings or shit. I'd be sitting on the floor, my head and shoulders collapsed onto the foot of Dale's mattress, and what I wanted more than anything was to be able to hold his hand, to hear his voice filling my head and feel the rhythm of his pulse. I thought about how to ask him for this; thought too much about it really. I said to myself: I want to hold his hand, is all, staring at my own hand placed casually across my leg, its veins, lines, and hairs. I don't want to *ask* to hold his hand: that is something different. If I have to ask, my desire will not be satisfied. I won't ask somebody to love me.

Near the end of August, Dale's dad came into town. He had planned to take Dale on a trip to Greece he was going on with his wife and step kids. They were leaving from Kennedy and he had business in the city anyhow. He took us out to dinner: Dale chose the White Horse Tavern, where Dylan Thomas died of alcohol poisoning. We sat out among the sidewalk tables, and I had a grilled cheese with bacon. Dale and his father ate steaks. Like Dale, his father was tall, threateningly broad in the shoulders; Dale's curly blond hair lingered only in traces around his ears and the back of his head. It became clear he did not expect Dale to become a writer. He had things to bequeath, unlike my parents.

My parents are happy, mostly, to have raised a poet, or rather, as Mom has it figured, a future professor of literature (God help me). My folks do not understand art, considering it, rather self-effacingly, beyond their scope. Sometimes they admire it—my mother taped all the Joseph Campbell inter- views off PBS, would tell acquaintances and friends that her son goes to the school where he taught. And sometimes they resent it—it took me away from home, away from them. Dale's father was different, used to the idea of art. Most especially to the idea of owning art, a thing of intrinsic, real, fiscal worth. He admires himself for turning a nice profit on a small Jackson Pollack more than he admires the dead guy who wasted his life splattering paint. "Do you still have the copy of *A Child's Christmas in Wales* I gave you?" he asked, examining the ancient wavy glass of the White Horse windows admiringly. Dale nod- ded, m-hmm. "You took the dust jacket off, didn't you? I hope you're not running it ragged, it took a lot of trouble to find that edition."

Dale's dad promised him Athens, promised him Crete. "If you'd like it better," he conceded finally, "you can go on your own next year, after graduation." Dale's eyes narrowed, he ate a french fry. "Something to do before you come back to Houston."

"I'm not going to live with you after school," Dale said.

"Of course not," his father responded, not caring to incorpo- rate Dale's tone into his interpretation of Dale's words. "Of course you'll find your own place."

"I mean I'm not moving back home, I'm not working for you."

Dale's father paused, chewing a large hunk of beef. "That's fine. There's no reason we have to make plans now. But I'd like for you to come with us next week. I've rented a boat, we can go fishing."

Dale left with him, two weeks before school started again.

Protesting, certainly, but he left just the same. I was alone in a bare, boxy apartment on Essex Street. My mother asked if I didn't want to come home until September. "No," I told her. "I want to use this time for myself." Putting all the shit Dale asked me to throw out into plastic garbage bags, I found his hidden stack of pornography: a *Penthouse,* a *High Society,* some others. Like in the old jokes, some of the pages were stuck together. I did not know that guys really did that.

Our senior year was different: Dale came back tan from Mykonos while I flashed the pearly white skin of a Lower East Side dweller, feeling out of health. John Dumphies was my suite mate and I fell asleep most nights hearing him strum his hippie guitar through the plaster walls, hearing him hump his hippie girlfriend every so often as well. Dale took poetry and the Russian Novel and The Philosophy of Technology. I took a different poetry, this time with a woman teacher, and The Bible and American History. I started going out with Tracey Sperber and, after Christmas break, Dale had an apartment in the city, scheduling his classes for two days a week. Tracey broke up with me and Dale said, "Good riddance. I couldn't stand that cunt anyhow." He wore a placid mask as he watched the changes flush over my face. "To tell you the truth, Jon, I bet she's a dyke after all." I thought about hitting him, I'll admit. But I didn't.

Tracey poked me hard in the back while I stood in the cafeteria line a few days later. "Where do you get off telling people I'm a lesbian, you asshole?"

I looked around: people looked back. Tracey was pissed, her eyes needling me, her hair pulled back tight. "I don't think you're a lesbian, Tracey. What the fuck are you talking about?"

"Dale told me what you said, you shit." She walked away from me, directly toward the ice-cream bar. At a very bad point for my reputation, she turned on her heel and snapped, "That's ballsy talk coming from Mr. Limp Dick." The anger in her eyes turned to amazement when she sensed the jovial reaction her comment had provoked among nearby tables. She suppressed a laugh. "And your poetry *bites*." Even I laughed then. She came back over and smacked me, still laughing, me laughing, though she hit me hard, the bitch. Walking away laughing, she flipped me the bird. I loved it. It was beautiful. That was almost graduation when that happened.

I don't regret anything, really, 'cause I think I learned a lot about who I am. But I wish I'd known for just a little while the things I know now. I'm not stupid for one, and I don't need to pretend to be. Just because my relatives aren't your professional, educated, intellectual sort of assholes. Just because I never got into philosophy and all I know about Hegel and Heidegger and Wittgenstein and Kierkegaard are their names. And only to say them, not even to spell them.

Dale and Foster used to argue this shit as if it were a rare pleasure. Metaphysical, epistemology, paranormatics, whatever. Pathetic fallacy, right? Sitting in the 21 room at school dances eating pretzels and having intellectual discourse while getting drunk. It wasn't not knowing the words that made me feel like there was something wrong with me—any moron can parrot back jargon from their philosophy professor. I felt stupid because I didn't give a shit. I could barely imagine what could interest me in the possibility of forming a totalizing system of ethics. Or solving the paradox of how do we know things. Two twenty-year olds, arguing over a tapped-out keg: how do we know things?

You just have to say, listen, there is at least one level of functioning, limited as it may or may not be, in which this is not a riddle but a self-evident fact: we know things because we perceive them rationally through our senses: I pump the tap and nothing comes out; I shake the keg and hear no sloshing sound. Thus I conclude there is no more beer. As for those other levels of reality and subjectivity, when we're all in Ph.D. programs and not drunk, we can consider them.

"Oh, but you're barely Cartesian," is what Dale said to that. "I'm way beyond you already."

Of course, now that I'm in a graduate program and not drunk, Dale is on smack, which is worse than being drunk. In either case he never admits that his mental functions are impaired. He's still a know-it-all, even when he's completely obliterated. It's a joust, a contest, that's got nothing to do with finding answers. I don't think Dale understands that yet.

I felt like I belonged somewhere, that people liked me. I wasn't wondering about the critique of pure reason. Now I realize that people didn't respect me maybe as much as I thought they did. Maybe I looked for respect from the wrong crowd. I had to get older and—I hate to sound too AA—sober to really get it. There are a lot of different kinds of people in this world and unless on some level you appreciate them as people, and not just figures in a metaphysical landscape, you're fucked.

—I'm sorry. That's not the expression I mean to use. "Up the creek" has the same meaning without the connotations of that last one: that submission, that homosexuality, whatever, equals the worst thing that could happen to someone. Being fucked, you know. I stop myself now, see, because I used to say things like that totally uncritical.

I'd call people "fag." Not gay people, of course—I was never that much of an asshole—but, you know, my friends or something when they were acting stupid: Dale, when he wanted to stay in his room and study when we'd planned to go rock-climbing that weekend. I never thought about it. There was this boy that went to school with us, Meecah Goldblum, and he was friends with some of my girlfriends, and sometimes they'd talk about how smart he was or how funny he was. I may have been one-tenth jealous but mostly I was interested. Because he sounded like an interesting person, someone that I'd like knowing. But he was gay, and I couldn't help thinking about it. The most fucked-up thing is the way my mind worked—I was convinced he was prejudiced against me because I was straight and he thought I was stupid, because he'd say hi to me sometimes without making eye contact and we never had a single conversation. Even when we were in a group he never looked at me.

I saw gay guys as having this superior attitude, like they were better, like everything I was into was far beneath their dignity. Honestly, I know how retarded this sounds now, but I felt like I was being snubbed. Everybody else liked me except for this kid who's talkative and friendly and funny when I see him across the room sitting with his friends, who won't open his mouth within ten feet of me. I took it personally.

I never thought of myself as homophobic or anything. I've got gay friends at Binghamton now, where I'm going to grad school. I mean, my friend Josh who's gay was talking about when we met, which was I guess about two semesters ago when we both took the Sartre/Camus/Genet seminar. He said to me, "Damn, that class when you started going off about the difference between faggots and real men in *Our Lady of the Flowers,* I thought you were the most phobic motherfucker . . ." I hadn't thought I'd said anything awful, I thought I was just talking about the book. I mean, Genet uses terms like that. And Josh said, "It wasn't what you were saying. It was the expression on your face, man. And the stutter?" And then he said, "I never thought we'd be friends," almost ashamed to admit he'd judged me.

His shame makes me feel like dog shit.

Josh says he is different from other gay guys, by which he mostly means that he looks like a normal guy with hair and jeans and T-shirts and he wears his wallet on a chain. He means he can't dance, and that he has a Batman tattoo on his upper arm. Not that there's anyplace worth dancing in Binghamton anyhow.

When we had known each other long enough for me to ask stupid questions, I asked him why he thought he was gay. We were in the driveway of the house where he had his apartment, me leaning against a cinder-block wall while he repaired some loose wiring on his motorcycle. "Like, why?" he chuckled, not even turning away from the recumbent BMW. "Like, too much estrogen in the womb or something? Hey, you've met my castrating mother, haven't you?"

"No," I corrected myself, acting casual and lifting a soda can to my mouth. "What feelings do you have that made you decide you're gay?"

"I fall in love with guys," he said, regarding me curiously with a grease-spotted face. "What else would there be?"

Everybody's got repressed urges, I guess. It's weird how conscious it is, really. I think every man feels some pull, some desire for other guys, not necessarily sexual. I've been what I guess you'd call in love with a couple of guys—Dale included, for a little while—but nothing ever strong enough to want to do something about. I don't get hard-ons from seeing some guy with a nice ass or anything. It's just sometimes when I have a friend I feel like I'd like to be close to him. It would be easy if I was just horny for cock. I'd hang out in the toilets at Grand Central or whatever. The downstairs library bathroom. But that's not what I want. If I could somehow manage a crew of cool fag friends to hang out with, drink with, sit up talking with, guys who were just like other guys except gay, then I know I'd roll over for some guy within the year. But even to Josh—I mean, he's nice-looking and everything—even to him, I'm this straight guy. Maybe he's wondered about me, but I'm his friend. He's not going to mess with me that way.

The usual path, as I understand it, is to go hang out at some gay bar and when a guy comes up to you to just talk normally about stuff and smile and flirt and maybe ask him where he got his shirt. You don't say, "I've never been in a gay bar before," or "you know, I don't really know if I'm gay and I'll go home with you but I might freak out and want to leave suddenly." I want to talk about these things. Example: say I run into some gay guy like Meecah from school at Vazak's where a lot of people I know hang out. Maybe I'll ask him what he's up to, and there's sort of a glazed sheen over his eyes, focused somewhere over my left shoulder, and I know he's thinking of the me he remembers from keg parties and loud conversations in the dining hall; and he tells me that he's doing some volunteer work, working as an AIDS educator or something, and I'll say, "I guess this isn't the best time in the world to be gay, huh?" He just drops me off with a murmured "well" and a shoulder shrug instead of letting me into this world I'm trying to get a grip on.

Okay, I'm not that subtle in my calculations and God knows I don't know what I'm talking about half the time, but I don't like the look I get when I say, "I think deep down, maybe everyone's bisexual." It starts to really piss me off, that look. All that fucking shit about gay brotherhood but it's all about drawing a line, one side's straight and the other's not and there's no use talking across it. Being gay's a party you have to crash, apparently. They don't invite you through the front door.

So I'm in a bar, looking at this kid Meecah, and I can hardly believe he's changed so much in three years. He even smiles sometimes, seems taller too. He tells me about the AIDS stuff he's doing, the writing he's been doing, and I'm telling him about grad school and my poetry workshop and shit like that. I'm getting drunk too, and after a really inept lead-in—God, he was talking about unsafe sex or something horrible like that—I say, "I've thought about sleeping with a guy before."

I might just as well have slapped him in the face, called him a cocksucking assmunch. "That's normal," he said. "That doesn't mean you're gay." Well, I'm not that hip on what's politically correct these days, but if wanting to sleep with guys doesn't make you gay, I don't fucking know what.

More daring: "Once I put the neck of a Rolling Rock bottle

up my ass," I told him. "And I thought it would hurt, but it didn't."

"Everybody does stuff like that," he said. "I wouldn't worry about it."

Man, do you not fuck, or am I missing something here? I thought about asking that for about five minutes, a question so loud in my own head I could barely hear him talk. Finally I just smiled and said I'd be seeing him. He just sort of nodded.

"Do you see Meecah Goldblum around much?" I ask Dale, who's lived in this neighborhood since we graduated. I'm still smarting from Meecah's intentional dullness, his vast unbreachable gayness, and Dale sort of grunts yeah, purposely dumb for his own straight reasons. "Who does he hang out with?" Dale mentions the name of a few girls whom I remember vaguely—"but I don't see him with people from school much." Guys, I offer, and he shakes his head, and that's as far as I push him. He seems put off by the topic.

I've had a couple Genessees before Dale arrived, and he's been to the bathroom twice before finishing his first beer, so I know he's on heroin again. He asks me if I'm writing anything and I tell him about a chapbook that me and Josh and this woman Sarah Posner put together—we did a reading at school that a lot of people came to, and Thom Gunn, whom I really admire, sent me a note complimenting me on one of my poems. Then Dale, who's had exactly one poem published in some East Village fanzine that I couldn't even find at St. Mark's Books, Dale says to me, "But nothing outside of school?," as if there's some sort of rich poetry scene I ought to be a part of in Binghamton, New York. It hurt me because I know he meant it to. But this is grad school. I'm no Frank O'Hara, but I'm twenty-four years old.

He feels a lack in this world, he says, off on his Melville trip again, a lack of heroism. People today shrink from living heroic lives, he says, and I slam my glass down. "Today on the news," I say to him, trying to control myself, "I saw people who risk being killed every day in order to bring medicine to injured children in Sarajevo. There are dozens of kids in this neighborhood who live in abandoned buildings and fight the police and the landlords and city hall to make a place for themselves to live. And haven't you ever heard of ACT UP, for crissake!" I yelled. "If you think sitting in your stupid room snorting dope and wondering where heroism's gone—wondering why there aren't any more white whales for white guys to chase—if that's what you're all about then you're a fucking moron. And your life is a big fucking zero."

"Fuck yourself, Jon," he says. "You can leave me the fuck alone if that's how you feel about me." He drank the dregs of his beer. "Why don't you go back upstate and leave me the hell alone?"

I won't leave him alone because I'm as full of shit as he is. I know that what Susan Sontag's doing in Bosnia is different from what Simone Weil did in Spain; that the squatters between C and D make this neighborhood a whole lot cooler for all the bohemian yuppies and dumbfucks like me and Dale; and I don't know shit about ACT UP or what they even do and only said it because I was thinking about Josh, and maybe

Meecah too, suspecting that if I'd tried to cultivate his respect instead of Dale's, I'd be someplace real different now.

And I know in any case heroism isn't about letting someone you've cared about destroy his life because you can't be bothered to relate to him anymore. I don't want to be like those guys on TV, the Normandy veterans they had on not long ago, dried-up old men talking about their best friend and meaning a dead kid fifty years younger than themselves. A ghost who disappeared ages ago. But things change so fast. "C'mon, Dale," I finally say, "I don't want to talk bullshit tonight. I just want to have a nice time with you. Is that all right?"

More Selected Lives in Brief

Mitch Huber

Mitch Huber lived with his mother and father and younger brother Kenneth in a yellow two-bedroom house in a working-class neighborhood of Newport News, Virginia. He was eighteen years old and unemployed, having recently enlisted in the army and having been discharged at boot camp for failing a drug test. He did this on purpose—took drugs before the test—because he was afraid of being sent to Bosnia or something instead of Germany or Panama like he assumed would happen when he signed up. The possibility suddenly seemed worth considering.

His brother Kenny was sixteen and still in high school. Sometimes Mitch would take Kenny and his friends out on weekends because Mitch had a car and Kenny didn't. And also because Kenny had one friend, Theodore Wedemeier, whom Mitch loved. Mitch had known Ted, through Kenny, since those boys had been thirteen or fourteen. Back then, Mitch had noticed, rather disinterestedly, that Ted possessed particularly refined features—not feminine, per se, but uncommonly well formed, along the lines commonly called "sensual," which means, literally, fleshy around the mouth and eyelids. But Ted was then still a boy, not obviously mature or self-willed, and did not offer Mitch much to think about. Mitch simply thought he had a nice face, and that this face would look equally well on a girl.

By the time Ted was sixteen, however, Mitch found Ted's charms specifically erotic. Ted was ballsy, violent, and sexual. He liked to talk about guns and kicking ass and treated Kenny like a weaker younger kid who didn't understand the rough ways of the world. Which was not completely inappropriate, since Ted came from a harder background and Kenny did like to roll in his immaturity sometimes, whining and sulking. Mitch imagined that Ted was, really, more on his own age level. Ted could hold his liquor and never threw up, while whenever they got drunk Kenny was always sure to.

Mitch felt certain that Ted liked him in a significant way, but he felt equally certain that a sexual relationship between them was impossible. Mitch didn't mind this so much, because he was sure that the qualities he found arousing in men would necessarily preclude them liking to have sex with him. So he contented himself with seeing how physically close he could get to Ted—how much sensory information he could collect to make his masturbatory fantasies more detailed and real-seeming.

By the summer of his being eighteen, Mitch had collected a lot of information. He could picture Ted naked without using much imagination to fill the gaps. They had swum and show-ered and wrestled together; once Ted had slept over with Kenny and Mitch saw him with a boner in his jockey shorts. This satisfied Mitch but it also bred a desire to take it further, to know Ted's feel and smell, etcetera.

Then one night when they were drunk, driving home from a party, Mitch felt up Ted's thigh below his cutoff shorts. Ted said:

"What are you, Mitch? A fag?"

and brushed his hand away. Mitch was ashamed, he had gone too far and violated limits he'd been well aware of. But then, after a considerable and painful pause, Ted added:

"I'll let you touch it if you do something for me."

Mitch was scared, anxious, frightened of a trap here. He did not respond right away, but only tightened his grip on the steering wheel.

"Seriously, man," Ted repeated. "I'll let you suck my dick."

Turning his head slightly, Mitch saw that Ted had pulled his penis, limp but fattening rapidly, out of the fly of his jeans. He was stroking it, and looking at Mitch. "Ah, shit," Mitch sighed. "Don't do that."

"I want you to blow me," Ted said, resting his hand on Mitch's leg.

"What do you want from me?" Mitch said. He was scanning the highway for someplace quiet to pull off, at the same time thinking he shouldn't.

"I'll tell you later," Ted said. "It's a big favor. You'll get more than a blowjob out of it."

Mitch thought to himself: I'm going to drive this car off the road in five seconds if I don't pull over. He said, "Okay." And breathed in deeply. "I want to do it."

He had never sucked a dick before. He sucked it, like a rubber nipple or a lollipop, hard enough to make Ted cry out and tell him to stop. "Rub your lips on it," Ted said, in a helpful tone of voice. "Don't be a vacuum cleaner. You want to jack me off, using your mouth."

"I've never done this before," Mitch said.

"Shit. You've seen it done, though. You've gotten blown before, right?"

"No," Mitch said. "I've never gotten one either."

"You want me to show you?" Ted said indifferently. "I can blow you."

"Are you sure?"

"Whatever, yeah," Ted responded. "Yeah, I want to."

Mitch got into his bed that night, finally, his anxieties misdirected by this experience of swapping blow jobs with Ted. He worried that Ted would tell someone that he had made a homosexual advance. That Ted could do this because people would believe him, and not believe Mitch that the encounter had been mutually desired.

Mitch all but forgot about the unspecified favor Ted said he'd request later.

So, when he was drinking orange juice in the kitchen of his parents' yellow two-bedroom house in Newport News, Virginia, dressed in a paint-stained T-shirt and cutoff sweatpants, at eleven o'clock in the morning of an early September weekday, he was not at all prepared for Ted to knock on the door, appearing sweaty and agitated, demanding that Mitch come with him.

Alarmed, he followed, silently, and rode in the passenger seat of Ted's stepfather's Oldsmobile back to the Wedemeier house. Ted did not speak during the trip.

Mitch followed Ted into the living room of the Wedemeier house. The coffee table was overturned and a newspaper's leaves were scattered on the floor. Mitch followed Ted into his parents' bedroom, and saw two bloody bodies sprawled theatrically, Ted's mom on the bed, her legs spread-eagled and her arms folded defensively around her head, Ted's father folded fetus-style on the floor by the nightstand. Both bodies were painted with blood, blood that was drying in the ears and hair and wrinkles to a chocolate-brown hue. Between Mrs. Wede-meier's feet, a curved pruning blade had been set down with care.

Mitch stood in the doorway, stunned, and rigid with apprehension.

"My dad used to fuck me in the ass," Ted said calmly. "And she"—he nodded toward his dead mother—"knew all about it. From, like, when I was eight or nine on."

Mitch's mouth sagged open.

"I guess I didn't have to do this," Ted said.

"I think I better go . . ." Mitch said.

"You're not fuckin going, idiot," Ted said.

Mitch stood and blinked for a while.

"Okay, Mr. Smart Boy," Ted said. "What do we do with them?"

Ted wasn't a mastermind criminal. Mitch wasn't so smart either. The bodies were heavy and the house was right on the street, close to other houses. The best idea was to take the bodies away and dump them, but Mitch couldn't figure out how to get them to the car without being seen. If they wrapped them up in sheets, the bodies would still sag like bodies while they carried them. There was a crawl space under the house but you still had to get the bodies outside. If they put the bodies into big boxes, neighbors would see and remember when the parents turned up missing—"We saw those boys carrying big boxes, must have been the bodies in there."

"I guess we could set the house on fire," Mitch said. "I can't figure how to get them out of here." Ted sat on the edge of the bed, a hygienic distance from his mother's foot, smoking cigarettes, one after another, and flicking the ashes on the floor, watching Mitch with an air of expectation. Mitch reflected on Ted's beauty, thought maybe it was all worth it. "You'd have to run away then. I mean, they'd discover that they'd been murdered. It wouldn't cover that up. But they wouldn't necessarily be able to tell you did it."

"Okay," Ted said, dragging in smoke. "We got a couple cans of gasoline in the garage."

"Wait," Mitch said. "Maybe we can do a little better." He took one of Ted's cigarettes and sat down on the floor. "You know," he said. "You're gonna have to blow me a hundred times to make up for this."

"Fuck that," Ted said, pretty casually.

"Are you serious? You think me helping you get rid of your murder victims is worth one blow job?"

Ted shrugged. "You can fuck me all day long if you help me get rid of them. I don't give a shit."

This was distracting Mitch from the problem at hand. "You'd let me screw you?"

"Yeah," Ted said. "I don't care. Listen, dumbfuck, why don't you think about the situation and you'll see I'll do just about anything you damn well want."

"Will you kiss me?" Mitch asked. Ted wouldn't kiss him when they were fooling around before.

"Yeah," Ted said, pushing some hair back behind his ear. "I'd kiss you."

"Will you kiss me now?" Mitch asked.

"Dammit." Ted frowned and shook his head. He ground out

his cigarette on the bed. "Do you wanna fuck right now? Let's go into the bathroom and fuck."

"Right now?" Mitch said with surprise.

"If you're gonna sit there and think about fucking me, let's do it now before my folks start to stink." Ted pulled his T-shirt off over his head and stood up, headed for the door. Mitch paused, confused, for a moment before following him. Ted was naked by the time he got to the bathroom; he grabbed Mitch by the waistband of his jeans and started kissing his mouth. It felt real, Mitch thought, like he really meant it. After kissing a while, he turned Ted around, took down his pants, and tried to stick it in.

Ted said: "Ow. Fuck!" It went in a little and Ted gasped and stiffened and said, "Take it out!" He turned around then and kissed Mitch's mouth again. "You got to eat me out some, I'm too tight back there." Mitch looked dazed. "You got to suck my ass a little," Ted said firmly, a little angrily.

When Mitch knelt down to lick Ted's ass, he brushed the cool porcelain of the bathtub and realized, with a feeling of sudden enlightenment, that they could dismember the corpses in it. But he kept it to himself until Ted said he'd licked his ass long enough and they fucked and came. What he did was jack Ted off while he fucked him and Ted stayed hard and sometimes clutched at Mitch's thigh, and when Mitch came inside him he held tight and made Mitch keep fucking and jacking until he came himself.

Ted turned around, his sweaty chest sliding against Mitch. He put a hand up to Mitch's face, kissed him and then, animal-like, licked at Mitch's teeth.

"Do you like having sex with men?" Mitch asked.

"It's all right," Ted said. "You're my friend and I appreciate that. You get what you give out, right?"

"If I fix this," Mitch said, "will you keep doing this with me?"

"Maybe," Ted said. "Will you get me a cigarette? I left them in the room."

Mitch stepped into his pants and pulled them up, buttoning them but not zipping up. He went back to the bedroom and saw Ted's Marlboros on the corner of the bed.

Those corpses were pretty well stabbed, he thought. They were dead people, he thought. They were alive this morning and now they were big, busted fat sacks of cooling flesh he had to figure out how to get rid of. Mitch had never seen them alive very much. Sometimes Mr. Wedemeier was drinking and watching TV in his special chair in the living room when Mitch dropped Ted off at night. He couldn't see Mr. Wedemeier's face now but Ted's mother was staring at the ceiling, a film of dried blood covering one eye and making it look like a dark hole into her head.

Mitch brought Ted a cigarette and lit one himself. "We're going to have to chop them up in the bathroom and take them out in trash bags," he said.

"Ahh," Ted said, scratching his pubic hair. "My hero." He put his hand out and rubbed Mitch's side, tenderly but also a parody of tenderness.

"You got a saw or something in the garage?"

"My dad has an electric knife in the kitchen . . ."

"No," Mitch said. "It's going to be wet. You got a handsaw?"

"Probably. In the garage. We'll have to look around."

"Well. Get one of the plastic runners from the living room and drag 'em into the bathroom so we can get started. I'll go look in the garage."

"Mitch," Ted said, putting his arm around Mitch's back. "You're a real pal. I appreciate this a lot."

"Put on some clothes you don't mind throwing out," Mitch said.

"You know," Ted said. "I like getting fucked."

"Seemed like it."

"Your brother don't, though," Ted smirked.

"Don't fucking talk about my brother," Mitch said.

"Well, he don't," Ted said. "I got him to let me once. Bet you couldn't a guessed that."

Mitch drew in a deep breath before picking his T-shirt up off the floor and putting it on. "There's a lot of things I couldn't a guessed," he said.

Mitch intended to make Ted do most of the cutting, but Ted got sick while he was sawing through his father's thigh bone and barely made it to the toilet to puke. He was near to fainting. So they took turns sawing, and both threw up often. It got to feel normal. Ted's mother had a deep gash in her side and a bulge of intestine worked its way out while they were dragging her. Mitch hadn't wanted to cut open the torsos because of the guts but she didn't give him a choice. When her intestine started leaking sour blood and shit, Ted convulsed and his vomit splattered across the vanity top, missing the toilet entirely. Then Ted started crying because he had killed his own mother. Mitch told him to shut the fuck up and stuffed Mrs.

Wedemeier's torso into a Glad heavy-duty trash bag. Mitch was only vomiting clear bile by then.

It took about nine hours to get the bodies thoroughly chopped and bagged. By then it was almost ten o'clock at night. They put the bags in the trunk of Ted's dad's Oldsmobile, along with a full gasoline can, and drove northwest. They got some gasoline and some coffee at a rest stop near Williamsburg, and Mitch cranked the stereo loud.

At about five-thirty in the morning, as daylight was breaking, Mitch spotted an abandoned farmhouse near Roanoke, Virginia. It was in pretty good shape, hidden in a grove of trees, with a For Sale sign by the road. Ted was asleep in the passenger's seat, and was briefly alarmed and disoriented when Mitch woke him. "Maybe there's a well here," Mitch said. "Or something."

They easily pried open a double-hung window off the front porch, and looked around. It was a big house, all the rooms wallpapered, with dark square patches where pictures must have hung for twenty, thirty years. It was pretty, in fact. On the second floor was a back hallway with lots of windows, a small child's bedroom with bookshelves and a window seat. "This is nice," Ted said. "This is my room."

"I'll take the big room in front," Mitch said. They knew they weren't really staying there.

There was a dusty root cellar in the basement, with wooden shelves all around. This was what Mitch was looking for.

"We'll put the bags in here, and set them on fire. They'll probably just bulldoze the house and never find anything."

He'd brought the gasoline especially to set the heads on fire. He thought they'd burn the heads in a little fire, like in an oil drum, then crush the skulls with rocks, throw the chips down a well or something. But he was very tired and this seemed like a good enough solution.

They drove away counting on the fire they'd started burning down at least a significant part of the house. Mitch was worried it might just go out without damaging the structure but it didn't seem likely, it didn't seem likely that anyone would search even a partially burned house's root cellar before tearing it down completely and bulldozing the site, and if all these unfavorable circumstances did happen it would take a long time to figure out who the bodies were.

They drove the car to Washington, D.C., and found the poorest, most criminal-looking neighborhood and abandoned the car in the scariest spot they could find. They were afraid even to walk away from it, since they didn't know D.C. that well, but they found a city bus and got on it and found their way to the Trailways station. They had planned to go back to Newport News but Mitch kept saying, "How are we going to explain your parents leaving? You'll have to report them, right? And then the cops'll question you. I'm afraid. We can't pull it off."

Instead of going home they bought two bus tickets to New Orleans, and arrived there destitute. Ted persuaded Mitch it was a good idea to hang around the bus station there, pretending to be half-asleep. Ted put his bookbag on his lap and had Mitch hold his dick underneath. The idea was for this to be semiobvious to anyone checking out boys in the bus station, and sure enough an older man came and sat near them, and began talking to them when Ted looked at him. The man offered to take them to a hotel if they would let him watch them do it. Ted said yes, and they went.

The man took them in a cab to the French Quarter. He had them wait on the street while he checked in, then came out and told them his room number. A few minutes later, they slyly sauntered in, sneaked past the desk clerk, and rode up in the elevator. The man let them in. Ted and Mitch made out on the king-sized bed. After a while the man lay down next to them with his head on his hand. Ted leaned over as if to kiss the man but instead grabbed him by the throat and clamped a hand over his mouth. Mitch punched the man in the head until he passed out, then Ted ran the bathtub to nearly full and they dragged him to the tub and held him facedown into the water until he stopped struggling, seizured, and died. They rummaged through his wallet. There was a couple hundred dollars there, and credit cards, but they were afraid to take the credit cards.

Ted and Mitch snuck out of the hotel, back to the bus station, and took a bus to Memphis. They found a single-room occupancy hotel there, downtown, and though it was dirty and small they could afford to stay there two weeks. Mitch thought they could find off-the-books jobs in Memphis, working in a warehouse or something.

They made up fake names for themselves, but no one would hire them, and they didn't hear about many jobs anyway.

Ted spent their last bit of money on some cocaine and snorted it himself. Mitch was very angry but pretended not to be. When Ted fell asleep, Mitch strangled him to death with a T-shirt. He thought Ted might do the same to him soon enough. He left Ted's body in the room, went out and mugged some guy, and bought a ticket to Portland, Oregon.

Over a few years living around the West Coast, Mitch became a crack addict. He got shot by another crack addict and died.

Nobody ever figured out what had happened to the Wedemeiers. Mitch was right about them knocking the house down without looking through the rubble. The fire department in Roanoke had thought it was just kids messing around in an abandoned house.

Sean M. MacDonald

Sean MacDonald was born in 1975 in Keelersville, North Carolina, educated in the Onslow County public school system, and admitted to the Savannah College of Art and Design in 1993, where he intended to study commercial illustration. During his first year at SCAD, he befriended two boys, Jonathan Muller of Charlotte, North Carolina, and Francis Reuben of Jacksonville, Florida, who shared his particular interests in rock music and hip-hop. Despite their limited experience as musicians—Sean and Jonathan could play the guitar and bass, Jonathan could keyboard a little, and Frank was accomplished only in playing violin—they soon put a little group together, inspired by, and in some ways bluntly imitative of, the popular New York trio the Beastie Boys.

Hopefully, one can imagine what the Beastie Boys would sound like with white Southern accents and the permanent addition of a hip-hop violin.

It might be surprising that they had some success with this act, but they did, playing local house parties thrown by fellow SCAD students, at first, and then in some local bars and clubs, as well as some in Jacksonville across the state line. At that time, there was a surprising amount of loose money build-ing up in the area—a curious coincidence of a general economic turnaround, the newfound suburban cosmopolitanism of a generation raised on cable TV and chain record stores and, lately, the Internet, and finally Savannah's transformation into a tourist mecca because of a best-selling nonfiction novel.

Most importantly for this specific story, John Waykes, an alternative-rock guitarist whose band had achieved critical notice and some commercial success in the late eighties, had married Emma Sothern Pocock, a Savannah native from a well-to-do family, and the couple settled there permanently in a three-story wood-frame Victorian house, a gift from Mr. and Mrs. Pocock, just outside of the downtown district. Having limited himself to the creation of serious-minded art-rock albums which reflected his truest vision of music in its intellectual purity, collaborating with other serious musicians of his era who had been left behind in the commercialization of "alternative" rock, Waykes thought of the small record label he founded in Savannah as a kind of amusing distraction.

When he saw MacDonald, Muller, and Reuben perform, by accident as it were, at a get-out-the-vote drive, he found them both amusing and distracting and introduced himself to the boys.

Overwhelmed by his having a reputation for being an actual musician with a commercial career, the boys were instantly impressed by his attentions. MacDonald called him "Mr. Waykes," and "sir," and, unlike his two friends, could not be persuaded with time to do otherwise. Waykes was thirty-seven. He determined that MacDonald had the most refined artistic sensibility of the three boys, and was also the silliest and most reckless, the most often drunk or drug-impaired.

MacDonald's recklessness annoyed Waykes somewhat more than it endeared the boy to him. He attributed his own failure to take real advantage of his commercial success, when he'd had it, as in part due to his indulgences in drugs and alcohol and this in part due to his fear of taking the process seriously, giving his all, and failing on his own terms. Waykes was temperamentally an asshole, and his arrogant superiority and palpable bitterness emphasized this, but he was a good-hearted man. He took an interest in Sean MacDonald and, by teasing and bullying him, and by plying him with liquor and invitations to come over and meet out-of-town visitors like former Hüsker Dü guitarist Bob Mould or Smashing Pumpkins singer Billy Corgan or independent producer Steve Albini—all of whom Waykes counted as friendly colleagues if not personal friends—Waykes managed to uncover Sean Mac-Donald's hidden handicap: his fear and discomfort with being homosexual.

In fact, Sean admitted in a bourbon-induced stupor, one reason he had started the group was because he had had a crush on Frank Reuben his freshman year and had used their common musical interests to machievel a friendship with him. Of course, now he knew, Sean said, that Frank was more or less straight and no potential love object. Waykes asked MacDonald where else he had looked for a boyfriend and Sean had nothing to say.

"So—you're not dating anybody," Waykes mused, "and you're supposing that all of your sexual feelings are going to go away because they're inconvenient to act on?"

"I don't know if I'd put it just that way, Mr. Waykes," Sean said, sitting Indian-style at the feet of Wayke's smoking chair in the side parlor, while the main party continued, smokeless but well lubricated, in the large parlor: Emma Pocock Waykes marshaled great social success out of being the Savannah deb with the rock-star husband. "It's just—I mean, whoever heard of a gay rapper, you know?"

Waykes laughed. "First of all—son—I don't know if I would call what y'all do 'rap' exactly." An Air Force brat from New Bedford, Massachusetts, Waykes made a point of adopting a Southern vernacular as a kind of phony homeliness. "And second, you might well be right that your kind of audience doesn't want to hear about you being gay—I think maybe having a boyfriend would be a better precaution against that than, say, sucking men off in a highway restroom, right?"

Sean stared down at the oriental carpet, ran a hand through his bristly brown, overdyed-blue, hair.

" 'Cause sex'll always get the better of you, ya know. That's a fact. It don't go away."

Sean still sat strangely quiet. Waykes flicked his cigar ash and tried to figure out why the boy was so sullen. John Waykes was not the guy anyone would pick ideally to enlighten a closeted gay twenty-one-year-old—he was really an asshole, and though some of his professional friends were gay he still thought of homosexuality as an essentially embarrassing personality quirk. But he was right in that he had seen lots of people do foolish things to avoid basic truths about themselves. His own marriage was a bit of a scam. Not that he was anything less than heterosexual, or that his love for Emma was in any way ingenuine, but he knew he lacked the fundamental capacity to subordinate his own ego to any feminine neediness, and had so chosen an equitably arrogant partner whose static and formal view of marriage often rendered the fact of an actual husband irrelevant to her.

Waykes had chosen to be Southern, in other words, in his marriage as well as in his speech.

"You're already doing it," Waykes said finally, as it dawned on him.

"Doing what?" Sean said.

"Drivin' your truck out to the rest stops."

"No," Sean said. "No, sir."

"No?"

"No, sir," Sean said.

Waykes sat back and swished his glass full of ice and watered-down bourbon. He sighed and put his cigar back in his mouth.

"It's more of a bookstore, actually," Sean said.

"Huh," Waykes said.

A couple of Emma's friends, a girl she'd gone to high school with and her lawyer husband, leaned in the doorway to tell John good-night. After opening the front door and seeing them off the porch, Emma herself leaned into John's "study." "Honey," she said, flashing her yellow-green eyes and pushing her straight blond hair behind her ears. She wore a pink sweater set, pearls, blue jeans, twirled her Doc Marten–shod foot girlishly. "Are you going to stay in here all night?"

"I'm just lecturing my protégé here, honey," Waykes said.

"I'm going to have to send Pete and Lawrence in here in a second, they're jonesing for cigarettes." She pronounced "Lawrence," another friend's husband, as if it were one syllable, "Luhnz." Sean did not understand the name from hearing it.

"Baby, they can go on the porch."

"John, it's fifty-five degrees out there."

"You're gonna make me open the window in a second anyhow."

She pshawed him and returned to her friends across the hall.

Sean was by now shifting restlessly on the floor.

"You're gonna do what you want, of course," Waykes said. "But you're a nice, clean boy, I can't see that what you want really is to be kneeling in week-old scum sucking some dick through a hole in the wall. Life doesn't just happen to you, kid. You gotta make things happen. If you wanna have somebody you gotta look for 'em."

And from that night, Sean MacDonald started to think purposefully about how he wanted to be gay and John Waykes started to think purposefully about whether he knew any decent-type homosexuals his age who could do a young guy some overall good.

He didn't want to offer MacDonald and his friends a spot on his record label until he was sure they wouldn't fuck him up businesswise by acting like dumbass teenagers.

When he saw the boys at a performance a couple weeks later, he overheard Jon Muller slyly tease Sean for being a faggot and he wondered if this meant Sean had told his friends or if it meant he hadn't.

He had, actually, and neither of them was very surprised. They'd pretty much known it since they'd met him. Frank

Reuben was Sean's roommate, they shared a big bedroom in a Victorian row house with beds on either end and a half-assed dividing wall built of a metal bookcase with stereo equipment, two dressers side by side, and an amplifier heaped with varying heights of secondary equipment as well as dirty clothes. Sean wasn't gay enough to be neat or smell nice. The three of them looked like boys you might hire to cut your lawn or paint your house, except for Sean's faintly blue hair and the rings stuck into parts of Frank's face.

Actually, though, that's what lawn-mowing and house-painting boys looked like these days, especially over the state line in Jacksonville. They liked the same music. It was a natural fan base. Waykes realized this. The boys were naturally funny but they were not essentially a joke band. They were pretty okay, really, and might be very good by the time they were twenty-eight or thirty. Being naturally funny could be the glue that would keep them together until they were technically proficient as well as calmly centered on some specific artistic goals.

Waykes wanted to see this managed right. He wanted to see if it were possible for creative teenagers, basically, to collaborate together and grow up well together so that in the end they could reap the rewards of this friendship together.

In his own case it had not been possible. From his old band, two of his former friends now worked, more or less lucratively, as studio musicians executing other people's ideas; and one had given up all musical ambitions after some failures and a drug problem and now taught high school English in New York City. None of them were very close at all and the last, Derrick Hall, the group's drummer, hated John now. Though John despised him quite as strongly—resentfully, since Derrick had spoken behind his back about John being a "user" and a "soul vampire"—whenever he had the occasion to feel this hate a miserable wave of self-pity would sweep over him and he'd wonder how their high school friendship ever came to this end.

They would get attention, these three boys, Waykes knew that much. This could be easily wasted if, by virtue of their immaturity, they each used this attention haphazardly, to soothe their own psychological sore spots. What one thought was a perfectly normal way to behave would look like foolishness to the other two and they would fight, their opportunity might be lost and they would remembered merely as some old group that used to play around Savannah and Jacksonville.

Waykes did not wish for Sean to use the band as an excuse not to develop his personal life, leaving these repressed energies to erupt violently and irrationally when the band was becoming successful and meeting movie stars and rock journalists. Waykes wished against this because it was what had happened with his friend Derrick. He had always thought that Derrick had no interest beyond his drum set. Because this suited him, because it made Derrick easy to work with and focused, John never cared that it seemed oddly incomplete. This was, apparently, what Derrick now blamed him for.

He would have liked to have introduced Sean to Derrick but he couldn't because Derrick hated him and lived in New York anyhow.

———

In Savannah, Emma knew a couple people from her college days at Oberlin in Ohio. Her college friends, indeed, had helped make her into the kind of person with whom John Waykes could fall in love—smart, well read, sardonic, with a residual cheerful pleasure in simple things like the smell of grass or cigarette butts, driving in a powerful but dumpy old car with an AM radio blaring, dirty jeans that fit comfortably, chocolate cake made from mixes late at night in a stoned frenzy, the sound and smell of an apartment building's laundry vents. This is what kept Emma from being an irritating provincial socialite. The previous year, a guy named Mark Erts had moved to town and Emma had seen him, gone to lunch a few times or ending up drinking can-beer out on the porch swing; and Emma had told John right off that this was okay because Mark Erts was "as gay as a bluebird."

She said this same phrase also of a couple which included a former high school boyfriend, Tony something and Alex something, but they were very upper-class and Savannah-like, in khakis held up by braided leather belts and neatly pressed and tucked plaid shirts and Shetland sweaters and male-hairspray-bottle-model hairdos and John could easily see the applicability of the bluebird simile to their insubstantial and flighty personae. They talked about redoing their sailboat and Alex's grandmother saying something amusing and suggestive about the old heirloom bedstead she'd given them and snippy things about racial demographics. They did not know John's music and he did not find them especially likable. On the other hand, Mark Erts was quiet and apparently mild-mannered, though the things he said mildly and quietly frequently sent Emma into seizures of laughter or horrified squeals. He wore jeans and workshoes and T-shirts, nylon or leather jackets slightly fashionable in their proletarian styling. His particular style of plain dress reminded John Waykes of himself. It seemed unstudied but John suspected it wasn't. Mark Erts's clothes said, I am a man but this is about as far as I'm willing to go to prove it.

He had lived in San Francisco for some time after college and had had a serious boyfriend with whom he had broken up painfully because the boyfriend had tested positive for HIV and was fixated on the idea that Mark felt sorry for him. They couldn't work through this problem very well because Mark did feel sorry for him, didn't know what he was supposed to feel instead, or in what other, less grating, way he could express this sorrow.

It may not sound like a big deal but it was.

Mark had lived for a year, single, in SF hoping that there might be a resolution which would reunite them, but after a year, Mark knew, he was simply being silly and immobile. He would not go to a gay bar because he worried the boyfriend would turn up, or some casual acquaintance, or simply a face he'd recognize to remind him of this earlier time, now lost. After a while, all of San Francisco reeked of shit, and Mark returned to Florida where he was from, got bored there in a month or two and moved a few miles north to Savannah.

Mark wrote short stories and was "at work" on a novel. John decided he liked Mark. He had problems, certainly, but John

thought they were good honest problems and not the fucked-
up kind that make you do bad things to other people.

This was not quite an honest evaluation on John's part.
Mark shared, to a noticeable degree, the same handicaps
of self-centeredness and defensive intellectual superiority
which had left their stamp on John's own life. But John liked
Mark's almost defiantly hapless attitude toward life, the nearly
complete channeling of all his egotism into his art, and—
maybe most of all—Mark's declarations that boys were stupid
and made no sense. John had been a boy so he knew. He had
never understood women's behavior either. He delighted in
the chance to see the baffling conflict of the sexes replayed with
no actual opposite sexes. It confirmed his view of human-
kind.

So when John had his next party, he invited Mark. He was
talking with Mark in his "study," filled, pretty much, with
smokers, since he and Emma had both invited guests. They
were joking about novelist David Foster Wallace and the blue
bandanna he was often photographed wearing. Mark said he
couldn't finish *Infinite Jest* but had read the book of essays. They
agreed, in consternation, that unlike the flamboyantly "Gen-
X" writers with their disjointed MTV prose and not-at-all-
incidental book-design style, Wallace had genuinely succeeded
in ripping off the real artistic lessons of eighties alternative
rock and punk.

Mark especially hated Wallace's bandanna, his "dew rag,"
because, Mark said, he always felt obviously phony when wearing one himself and wondered why Foster didn't. John was
pleased by this and laughed. "Dew rag," he repeated.

And then Sean MacDonald walked by. "Oh, here's MC MacD, the great white hope of Savannah's hip-hop scene," John declared, grabbing Sean's arm.

Sean stopped, smiled trustingly, his eyes wide.

"Mr. Waykes, sir," he said. "Thanks for inviting us to your party."

"Not at all," John said. "I need to introduce you to your future boyfriend."

Mark snorted, accidentally dropped the inch-long ash of his cigarette onto Emma's grandfather's Turkish carpet. They'd made eye contact; Mark was embarrassed.

"I'm not at all kidding," John said. "Take me seriously."

"MC MacD," Mark said, holding his hand out elegantly. "I'm Mark Erts, I'm a friend of John's wife."

"Call me Sean," Sean said. "MC MacD" was John's laughable invention.

"A half hour on the porch swing," John said, nodding toward the front-facing window of the narrow room. "And no petting. Your mother and I are watching."

Sean and Mark regarded each other uneasily. Sean was smiling, aware that he was being made fun of but unsure whether this was good-natured or not.

"I didn't say this was up for discussion," John said. "Porch swing."

Sean shrugged, grabbed the sleeve of Mark's shirt, and led him towards the door into the hall. "Whatever you say, sir."

John stood for a second, turning his attention to the big crystal ashtray by his chair. There was a cigar end big enough to light again.

"That 'sir' shit is getting kind of irritating," he said. "Who am I supposed to be, fucking Peppermint Patty?" He was talking aloud but to no one in particular. Across the hall, Emma moved her hands in lively conversation, half seated on the arm of a sofa. John waited to see how long he could stare at her before she noticed. It took a count of nine.

George Gordon Plowhees

Geordie Plowhees drives to work. He is nineteen years old. He works at a bar, it's his second job. During the day he apprentices at a custom cabinetry workshop in Fell's Point. His girlfriend doesn't work, she takes care of their daughter. She is not real good at it. She used to complain that Geordie didn't bring home enough money but then he found his job at the bar and now she doesn't complain. When he comes home Thursday and Friday and Saturday nights around three A.M. with his tips he hands her a big bundle and she counts it and puts some in a cookie jar and some in her purse and sometimes she puts some aside to pay their friend Paul for the pot he sells them on credit.

The parking lot of the bar is next to the Maryland State Penitentiary. Sometimes Geordie sees armed guards walking right on the other side of the chain-link fence. The thing he dislikes most about his job is worrying that one night an escaped convict or dope fiend will carjack him. It's never happened to anyone as far as he knows but it seems likely. If it happens anywhere, that parking lot sure looks like a good place for it to happen.

He has his backpack on the passenger seat next to him. It usually holds a change of T-shirt and an extra pair of jeans, a couple pairs of white sports socks, a pair of white thong underpants, a white fishnet G-string, some Band-Aids, and a Brut stick deodorant. Sometimes some money and some cigarettes, an ATM receipt or a pack of Big Red chewing gum, some napkins from McDonald's.

Geordie hates the fishnet G-string. It's uncomfortable and leaves his dick totally showing. He has to pull on his dick when he's dancing, to keep it from shrinking up into his groin. The bar's not all that warm. That G-string gets him the most tips, though, because it does show off his complete dick. Like navel oranges in their plastic mesh bags, an interesting piece of produce to inspect.

Another dancer, Mark Burney, who calls himself Marco at the bar, makes the fishnet ones. Geordie picked the white one because it looks the most like athletic gear and with his thickening body the athletic-gear stuff looks appropriate on him. Mark charged him ten dollars. Mark says the straps are elastic but Geordie thinks they're really just office-sized rubber bands. They chafe. He can feel the strap slide to one or the other side of his asshole, which he doesn't like to think of as having an outward physical presence. It's supposed to just be a hole to shit out of but the strap makes him aware of its moundlike, vulvalike, quality.

Sometimes a customer will talk to him about how they can see his asshole and if they say things especially dirty about it it puts him in a bad mood for the rest of the night. If they call it something ridiculous or snicker about how they suppose he uses it.

Johnny Ford calls Geordie Miss Butch because he can be sensitive about men talking dirty to him. Johnny calls himself Johnny at the bar. It says "Johnny" on his chest, in blue-black script, so he doesn't have much choice. Johnny is more or less a real whore, and a real queen, but he is also a very tough boy. Geordie gets scared, sometimes, for the men who pay to blow Johnny in their cars after closing.

Johnny's never robbed a customer that Geordie knows of, but if any of the boys were to do it, Johnny would be a good one to expect to.

All the dancers are more or less gay boys, despite what might be fun to think about them. Geordie is more or less a gay boy but he doesn't like older men, he likes guys his own age and he likes them to be his friend and not so much boyfriends. Geordie loves his girlfriend too. People are like that. You can't tell a lot just by who someone has sex with. I can't explain it for you.

Geordie hopes that the customer he hates won't be in tonight. It's this guy named Matt, probably twenty-five or twenty-six and not a bad guy really, in fact Geordie liked him at first and that's why he hates him now. He doesn't show that he hates him. Sometimes he doesn't admit that he hates him. It's just become creepy how regular he comes in, how eager he is to talk to Geordie, and how blatantly, now, he snubs the other dancers.

Matt never touches more than his legs or his butt cheeks, and he touches very casually—almost perfunctorily, as if the touching has no relation to sexual lust but is merely what one does when one addresses a go-go dancer. He usually will look Geordie in the eye when they talk. It's cool to pick a customer or two every evening to talk to like a real person but Matt won't go away; Matt's picked Geordie now and Geordie likes to do the picking.

Matt has lingered to closing time, watched the dancers jump behind the bar precisely at two A.M., retrieving their clothes from whichever hiding place they're using and taking a very few seconds to find their jeans and T-shirts and sneakers. They sweep up, empty ashtrays and all. Matt has heard the other guys call Geordie Geordie and not Brian, which is the name he tells the customers. It's not supposed to happen but it does. Geordie started to hate Matt the first time Mark Burney slapped him on the shoulder on his way out, said, "Night, Geordie," and Matt smiled, made eye contact, and called him Brian right in the next breath. Like they had a secret together which Matt was agreeing to keep.

Tonight the only thing different going on when Geordie walks in the door is that some boy is talking to Tom, the manager. This boy, Geordie gathers quickly, wants to dance here. He has, Geordie hears him say, never danced before but he thinks he'd be good at it. The boy is good-looking enough and holds himself like he has a nice body but he's a little too scabby, Geordie thinks. There's something not quite right about it. Stashing his bag over where Mark usually stashes his—away from Matt's preferred corner—Geordie keeps listening.

Geordie decides that the new boy is straight and fucked-up somehow and thinks this job will get him a whole lot of money fast. Probably thinks it will give him an opportunity to hustle. This makes Geordie a little depressed already. Johnny's hustling doesn't depress him because Johnny is a slut, Johnny enjoys sex with men and manages to blur any fixed distinction between merely picking up guys and milking them for money. Mark is even better, Mark will, rarely, tell some especially cute guys who've come in a group about an all-hours dance club or something and agree to "maybe" meet them there after closing and he will get what's apparently a boyfriend out of this, and even Johnny can't say whether Mark's hustling the guy or not.

"I been on the bus for a couple days, from San Francisco," Geordie hears the boy tell Tom. "Come to stay with my brother."

"Well, you can't wear those socks on my bar. Come in a little earlier tomorrow with some clean clothes and we'll see what you got, okay?"

"Come on, man. I don't know if I can come back. Gotta make some money somehow."

Geordie looks over. Customers will be coming in in maybe another twenty minutes or so. Johnny's wormed his way over to the discussion in his usual con-artist fashion, says, "Come on, Tom. Listen, I got a extra pair of socks you could wear. Come on, man, I'll fix you up." He has his hand on the new boy's shoulder.

"Thanks," the boy says.

"So what's your name?" Johnny asks the boy, guiding him toward the bathroom.

"I'm not promising anything," Tom says harshly. Geordie doesn't hear the boy say his name. Maybe he doesn't.

Mark comes in, discovers Geordie usurping his clothes-stashing spot. He laughs. "Hiding from your boyfriend, man?" Mark says, meaning Matt. They've talked about the whole deal. Geordie shrugs. "You could tell him to fuck off."

Geordie shakes his head. "I don't want to tell him to fuck off."

Mark laughs. "He used to be a good tipper, that guy. Until he fell in love with your ever-broadening ass. Shit, what do you weigh these days, anyhow?"

"Shut up," Geordie says. "One ninety." A few weeks ago, Tom had told him to stop doing chin-ups on a steam pipe that runs over the bar.

"You want I could tell him it's my birthday." That was a ploy Mark liked to use. It simulates a personal revelation and gets you more tips in one neat gesture.

"Son of a bitch!" Johnny slams the bathroom door, holding his face in one hand. "Tom, call the fucking cops."

"What the fuck, J?" Tom says, wiping the bar.

"This kid's a freak, man, this kid's a junkie or something, he's messed up, he fucking punched me."

"What'd you do to him?"

"Me? What'd I do to him? Me? Jesus fuck."

"Calm down, J."

"He's all like holed up in the stall, man, with his feet against the door! Fucking Christ!"

Geordie and Mark exchange a silent, apprehensive look.

"What'd you do to him, Johnny?" Tom's used to regarding Johnny as a borderline hysteric but tonight he looks genuinely angry and distressed and Geordie sure believes something bad just happened if Johnny says to call the cops.

"I fucking told him," Johnny says, in his prima-donna voice, "that he smelled like shit, Tom. That's what I did, for your information."

"Huh?" Tom laughs.

"I'm fucking serious, man. I was trying to help him out, gave him my fucking extra socks, was gonna lend him one of my fucking strings, man, but when he took off his jeans I was like, shit, man, you fucking take a dump in those drawers? Man!"

"Huh," Tom says, immediately more serious.

"He got track marks all over the place, man. Fucking got that junkie constipation odor in a brown Pig-Pen cloud around him. I'm like, no way, man, you can't come out here and dance smelling like ass. And he like—freaked the shit out on me, man."

"Calm down, J." Tom says.

"He fucking shoved me, real fucking hard. He don't smell like shit, he says. I think I got a concussion or something from that fucking hand dryer of yours, man—get some fucking paper towels already, it's not 1970. Now he's fucking barricading himself in the fucking stall."

"Christ," Tom says.

"Good luck to him is what I fucking say. Maybe he can shit the whole thing out this time, man. Fucking junkie."

Tom doesn't want to call the cops, particularly.

Geordie and Johnny are underage, not for dancing but for working in a bar with a liquor license. You're supposed to be twenty-one to serve. The cops won't shut the place down but they might give him a fine and make him send Geordie and Johnny home. Which would piss off Geordie's girlfriend, for him to come home with no money.

Geordie says, coming out from behind the bar, not bothering to put his sneakers back on, "I can probably talk him out."

Johnny says, "I wouldn't try it, man."

But that's because Johnny ends up physical-fighting in almost all confrontations. Last week he almost fought a customer for handling his dick without tipping him well enough first. Geordie knows himself to be a calm and reasonable person and he wants to get through the night without seeing a cop.

"Prop the door open," Tom says. "Geord, maybe you better not."

"Let me just give it a shot," Geordie says.

Tom looks annoyed and upset. It's too close to opening time for the cops to come and get the boy and leave without customers seeing, and customers really hate seeing cops. Still, Tom is a decent-enough guy and doesn't want anything bad to happen.

What's happening is that this kid is, actually, holed up in the bathroom stall, one foot visible and the other, apparently, holding the door shut. Tom is following behind Geordie, standing at the bathroom door and watching carefully. A pair of jeans is on the floor by the sink and they are blue but look gray. Much more than one bus ride's worth of not washing. They smell musty but not especially like shit per se. But then, Tom and Geordie are smelling them at five feet's distance, almost.

What's happening is that this kid is crying in there. Crying, and angry.

"Hey, man," Geordie says in as gentle a voice as he can manage, the voice he uses on his daughter. "What's up in there?"

The free foot lifts up and disappears, reinforcing the door.

"I don't smell like shit," says the teenage voice.

Geordie swallows, blinks, looks at Tom.

"Fucking faggot," the boy says.

Meaning Johnny, presumably. Johnny scowls from the darkness of the barroom, a few feet past Tom's shoulder. Tom makes a "what's up?" kind of gesture, which Geordie ignores. He tries to see the kid's face through the space between door jamb and door but the kid must be hunched forward because all he sees is a shoulder.

"You want your jeans, man? You wanna get dressed?"

Geordie goes over and picks up the boy's pants, hangs them over the side of the stall. "I'm gonna have a smoke, you want one?"

Geordie shoots Tom an expectant sideways glance; Tom reluctantly hands him him his own pack, and lighter, from his T-shirt pocket. Geordie makes a point of fumbling with the lighter, letting it flint without lighting a couple times, so the kid knows he's for real.

The jeans finally disappear over the wall, and the feet come down. Tom mouths the words "push it," meaning the stall door, but Geordie doesn't.

The feet are standing on the floor, stepping into the jeans. The jeans zip and the door slowly opens. The kid looks sourly at Geordie—penitent but peevish. He takes the cigarette Geordie offers without a thank-you and cocks his head to receive the light. He runs one hand over the rim of his ears as if—Geordie thinks—he's used to having long hair that needs to be swept away from lighters, rather than the brush cut he's got going.

He does smell like his ass is dirty, like some nasty third-grader who doesn't know how to wipe himself properly.

Geordie just stands there with him for a few puffs. The kid's blue eyes are set in puffy, red skin like he's been crying. Geordie thinks, ironically, the boy looks a lot like Johnny, if shorter and smaller.

I mean—that's what Geordie thinks: that this is ironic.

"Do you have any place to go?" Geordie asks.

The boy shakes his head.

"Well—uh—you gotta go somewhere, you know. You gotta take off. I don't want to be uncool, but—"

" 'S okay," the boy says.

Johnny splits from where he's been hovering; Tom stays put, but stays silent. The boy comes out, retrieves his socks, which are pure black on the soles, and precisely foot-shaped, stuffs them into his pockets and, without stooping, knocks his sneakers upright. He wiggles his feet into them.

"Listen, man," Geordie says. "How 'bout twenty dollars? Would you take that?"

The boy's eyes are on his feet. Geordie produces a folded-up bill from his jeans pocket.

"It's from me—okay?" Geordie taps himself on the breastbone. "All right? You'll take it."

The boy does snatch it, without comment, and puts it into a pocket where it can nestle with a loathsome blackened sock.

Once Geordie has him out of the bathroom, the kid breaks into a trot, then a full run, to the bar's front door. For a moment, Geordie freezes with fear, thinking it'll be locked and the whole scene will have to start over. But the bouncer has arrived and unlocked it already; the kid pushes straight through and is gone, probably flying down the street into the night. The bouncer's name is Johnny but is much older and fatter than "dancing Johnny," which is how he refers to Johnny Ford to distinguish himself. Bouncer Johnny peeks around the door into the barroom, a quizzical expression on his face.

No one bothers to explain it to him.

They all stand around looking for a long while, until standing around looking becomes ridiculous. Then everyone starts to do their regular stuff, Geordie goes into the bathroom to wash his hands, Tom's in there spraying Lysol everywhere and Mark sidles up to Geordie, leans against a sink, waiting for the dirt, an oral report. Geordie just looks at him, smiles wanly, and sighs.

Mark gives him a quick dry kiss on the side of the forehead, stands up, rubs him on the back, and leaves Geordie alone there. Well, not alone—Tom's still there, Lysol can hissing at the toilet stall. Geordie looks at himself in the mirror.

That's How Straight Boys Dance

Homosexuals, according to Jeff's straight friend George, have always been exceptional *readers,* but in fact only recently have we actually been writers, homosexual writers, so at the present we still read better than we write.

"Most fags are boring as straight people—they start businesses with lovers and end up in Hollywood, Florida, with dogs and doubleknit slacks, and I have no desire to write about them," wrote Andrew Holleran's narrator in *Dancer from the Dance.* All for the best since the double-knit-slacked businessmen in Florida are not readers. They may read. That very book which excludes them in its preface may sit on a walnut-finished bookshelf; they may have read it in the summer of 1983 lying out on a beach blanket in the backyard with a pitcher of Long Island iced teas. But they are not Readers in that larger cosmological sense by which, in the same way others divide the world into Homo- and Heterosexual, George and Jeff divide the world into Readers and Nonreaders.

"English and Math," George says, correcting the proper terms for this divide of consciousness. "By the time you're in junior high school, you know whether you're English or Math: you make your choice.

"Most people are Math. I'm not saying they like math, or necessarily are good at math. It's the promise of math that gets them. Math's an abstraction, we both know that, a series of arbitrary symbols, a series of postulates and theorems which can't be proven except by self-reference. But how does math present itself? As truth, as readily understandable objective truth: all you've got to do is learn to do it."

George fumbles for a moment, selecting examples to clarify his thoughts. "Galileo, Da Vinci, Einstein." He pauses. "The great math radicals of history. They could see something else in that system, something potential." He coughs a little. "They put Galileo in jail. When Einstein was in grammar school they thought he was retarded.

"People want to know, to know things for sure, and that's what Math gives them, even if what they know for sure is they're going to be assistant manager of a Dairy-Mart, have a fertile wife who was their tenth-grade girlfriend, and live half a mile from their parents."

And Jeff says, "So what's English?"

George falls back in his chair, exhausted. "Don't be an idiot, man." His arm lolls over the edge of the low seat, fingers dragging on the rug. "You know what English is."

This is New York: Jeff and George are both twenty-two and have fled here from disparate circumstances. George's father was a petty diplomat, and he's lived in Tokyo, Ottawa, Laos, Chevy Chase; George and his family parted ways as his father was reassigned to Bucharest after the fall of the Iron Curtain. Jeff's from the country outside Baltimore, a town where his family's lived for nearly two centuries while neatly avoiding the distinction of gentility. He went to a high school with the indecorous name of Cowtown, in recognition of the area's wealth of dairy farms.

"When I was seventeen or eighteen," Jeff recalls, "I'd decided that I'd never felt loved or approved of by my father, and because of that I was destined to search for love and approval from other men." Jeff sits in a chair like a contortionist, right foot under left buttock, elbow on knee, head tilted forty-five degrees. "It was a combination of bad psychotherapy, Gay Studies—and the realization that five-foot-six blond pretty boys couldn't, even on the most subconscious level, represent my father—that convinced me otherwise. I haven't replaced it with a new theory or anything. I've just gotten to the point where it's okay for me to say I don't have any clue why people are gay, if it even makes sense to say that particular 'people' are 'gay' which, again, I'm not sure of.

"Freudian psychology says that homosexuality is a developmental stage that should be outgrown, replaced by 'normal' genital heterosexuality. Well, I liked to wear my sisters' and my mother's clothes when I was little, and I liked to pretend I was a girl. Needless to say, I learned quickly what society thought about that." Jeff quickly downs the rest of a glass of iced tea, the amber liquid swirling in the bottom of the glass.

"I assumed for the longest time that I did that, played with dresses and all, because I was a prepubescent homosexual. That as soon as I was mature enough to think of sexuality as sex, I stopped and thought of myself as gay instead of a failed girl. I've matured to genital homosexuality, understand?"

Jeff stuffs his hand into the tight pocket of his jeans, pulling out a crushed pack of Camel Filters. "Still nobody talks about this. I've talked about it with my gay friends and all, and some of them did the same things. But maybe some boys who are straight did too. We don't talk about that." It takes one, two, three matches before his cigarette is lit. "It was a part of me that was taken from me before I knew how to think about it."

Jeff was a textbook case of gender identification disorder, Yale psychiatrist Robert Green's "sissy boy."

"Oh, fuck that." Jeff inhales deeply while adjusting the rubber band of his ponytail, his sublimated femininity. "Actually, it's not the least bit sublimated. What's femininity anyhow? Are you one of those gender reifiers? I have long hair because I couldn't have it when I was little.

"I wore dresses, for sure. I had one that was blue with a gingham apron, just like Dorothy Gale, which is the closest I've ever come to a Judy Garland fixation, by the way—but I had to wear hats, play wigs, I could never get the hair."

Jeff places the cigarette in a glass ashtray, one he'd taken from his grandparents' house: it bears a family crest etched, in mirror image, on the bottom. "I don't want to be a woman. Or a drag queen. It was never something I did for attention, to get people to look at me. I did it for myself.

"People say that gay men act effeminate because society sees men who sleep with men as effeminate. I hadn't slept with anyone when I was three fucking years old, okay? I didn't cross my legs too high up in grade school to receive all the lovely attention I got from it." Jeff's body is curved elegantly in the armchair, an elegance that a twenty-two-year-old body might possess that an underweight eight-year-old surely wouldn't. "I let it be driven out of me, first by my parents and the straight people around me, and second by gay boys spouting bullshit about men loving men as equals, meaning you have to act like a 'man.'

"I mean, who the fuck wants to act like a 'man,' anyhow?" He turns in the direction of his silent friend, sprawled on the springy couch. "George, you want to act like a 'man'?"

George stirs only slightly, like the famous dormouse. "If I acted like a 'man,' I'd have to date a girl who acted like a 'woman.' "

"As it is, George doesn't date much of anyone. My friend Kendra, incidentally, on hearing of an activist group called 'Men of Color with Men of Color,' proclaimed herself founder and sole member of her own group, Girls of Color with Nobody of No Color. There's a sex drain among New Yorkers around our age. Nobody's getting laid."

"People are getting laid," George protests. "It's just not us."

"Well, I won't say I have better things to do," Jeff says, "but I manage fine without it, most of the time. I'm going through a period of recovery. The guys I've been with in the last two years have thought either I'm too radical or too conservative.

I'm not conservative, certainly, but I'll also say I'm no radical, at least not in narrowly defined terms. I'm a left-winger, certainly. Radical means 'root,' however, so strictly speaking, a radical gay perspective would be one that saw a dichotomy of sexuality as the fundamental human difference. And not even being sure of the categories of 'gay' and 'straight,' I can't be a gay radical."

"He's a radical English," George offers.

"I'm a historical materialist," Jeff corrects him.

"You're a historical materialist wanna-be, buddy." George puts on his black-framed glasses. "Call me back when you've read more than a fucking Marx *anthology*."

"I may not have read a lot of Marx," Jeff confides, "but I'm up on contemporary theory. Anyhow, I don't believe in sexuality as a natural category. Which makes me ideologically incompatible with most people." George and Jeff share an apartment on the barely gentrified fringes of Brooklyn's Park Slope: one floor of a 1870s brownstone, with fifteen-foot ceilings, picture moldings, and marble mantelpieces, and three rubbish-heap upholstered chairs, which sit in the center of the main room like a miniature Stonehenge.

From the child-psychology books he surreptitiously thumbed through (mostly cruising for anatomy illustrations) and from *Donahue* episodes he caught on the days he pretended to be sick, Jeff acquired a halfhearted fear that his mother would accidentally burst into his room and find him in her silver-and-aqua empire-waisted ball gown with her rose-plum lipstick and charcoal-blue eye shadow, his shaggy brown hair fluffed up with a mothball-scented quail-feather ornament he'd stolen from her cedar chest. This fear, plus the feel of the stiff fabric smelling of Evening in Paris, got Jeff aroused; he'd invariably jerk off, naked save for a strand of pearls and panty-hose rolled around his knees, stroking his body in front of the mirror, the dress neatly draped across the baby blue quilt on his bed.

Every year, around September or October, Jeff's father would need to have new suits made. When Jeff was three or four, and his father spent the summer away in Charlottesville, getting a master's degree in business administration, it was only one suit, a gray moderate-weight generally appropriate year-round. By the time Jeff was ten and eleven, his father could afford four new suits made up annually. Jeff was permitted to choose the lining. Thus, at age fifteen when he helped his mother pack up his dead father's closet, dividing the suits into three piles— Consignment, Goodwill, or Keep for Jeff—he could date them by the silky fabrics inside the jackets. Orange and Blue polka dots, circa 1974; Horse and Riders on blue silk, circa 1980; a visual history of Jeff's developing taste.

The ones he kept required considerable taking in, and Jeff just wore them for fun, mostly; the pants, if you pleated the waist, would fit fine, but the jackets were always still too big, and those pieces were too complicated to readjust on his mother's sewing machine.

Jeff was just starting to appreciate suits by 1985, when his father died, but he'd always liked clothes. His mother's every-day clothes, wraparound skirts, turtlenecks, or, when she was young and her husband owned only a few suits, a homemade blue housedress with red gingham trim—these he knew intimately but never thought about. The dresses she kept either at the back of her wardrobe or in a box in the basement, these were the ones Jeff coveted.

He was thirteen or so before he was actually left alone in the house with those dresses, and he waited twenty minutes after the taillights had disappeared from the driveway before running downstairs and making his selection.

"I was also beginning to read at that age," Jeff explains, "that is, novels and such. I'd put away my books on mummies and the kings and queens of England, which I'd initially liked for the paintings of dresses anyhow. There were three things I learned from my cursory readings of American literature: that teenage American boys were all straight, but indulged in painful platonic relationships; that they were all white, Protestant, and upper-class." Jeff raises his eyebrows, smiling. "And they all attended Eastern boarding schools—which I promptly aspired to, soon as I figured out where some were." Even at fifteen, Jeff was never naïve enough to suppose that these were the only boys that existed, but it did seem they were the only literary kind of boys, the only boys worth writing about, if one was to write.

Jeff's art teacher was Mr. Freedman, a hippie Burl Ives who had pulled out his teeth with a pair of pliers when he was fourteen, he claimed, because there was nothing else to do in his tiny Pennsylvania hometown which was even smaller than Cowtown. Mr. Freedman had seen an intriguing denture advertisement in the newspaper that inspired his self-surgery. He clicked the plates around in his mouth, audibly, in the pause after the story. He believed there was always some out for frustration, whether it was artistic creation or self-mutilation.

["A lesson I've learned well," Jeff affirms. "Each of these holes"—he tugs on his ornamented earlobes—"are detoured suicide attempts. There's five of them, see?"]—which leads to Freedman's other famous saying: putting two fingers together, letting out a high-pitched squeak one could not have expected from his stout innards, he'd say, "This is the world's tiniest violin playing 'My Heart Bleeds for You.' " Romantic troubles, tension at home, lost homework, creative block: Mr. Freedman's heart would bleed for you, sometimes on the world's smallest record player rather than the violin.

He let Greg Heeler make, as his ceramics project, what definitely turned into more of a bong each class period. Jeff was vaguely frightened of drugs (then), and drug users; and being in a class with a known stoner caused him a bit of anxiety. Kristen Eckert, a teased-up blonde in pretty pink and blue sweaters, sneered at Jeff across her desk. "Doesn't he *know* what that is?" Jeff gave the half-smile and shrug he used to steer clear of potentially difficult conflicts. Greg grinned a ratlike smile from underneath his long, shiny hair, leaning back in his chair in admiration of his finished product.

"That's wonderful," said Mr. Freedman, rocking rhythmically, hands on hips. "Beautiful lines. And it's so smooth, so symmetrical, I can't believe you've never worked in clay before." His thick sausage fingers ran over the mouth of the tube, gently, in admiration, until that horrible moment when he shifted his weight onto that arm. The clay oozed in turdlike filaments through his separated fingers.

Freedman's high, tittering laugh emerged. "Oops!" He drew back, shocked. "Well, it's just as well, considering. Couldn't let it be said I let students make paraphernalia." Greg's jaw dropped, and the hair fell from his eyes as he raised his head in amazement; they were small, wet, blue—Jeff had never seen them exposed before. "Mr. Freedman . . ."

"Squeak. Squeak." His back was turned, walking away. "My Heart Bleeds for You, Greg." Freedman's cynical silliness was funny, but also fearful. He'd sometimes forget he was dealing with children, and accidentally stomp an ego, or set off a bitter rivalry in the midst of the fragile alliance that was Studio Art Three. Greg was a mean stoner boy who told stories about tying cats to clotheslines by their tails and making them fight, burying them to their necks in the dirt and running over them with the lawn mower, or, most classically, sticking a firecracker up a fat tom's asshole.

["My grandfather told me the same story when I was little," Jeff notes. "In his green vinyl easy chair. Except he called it a nickel firework. Rednecks are evil, by the way."]

In junior high school Greg hung small nerdy boys by their shirts on coatracks. Jeff's deskmate Steve was exactly that kind of small nerdy boy, with enough of a social persona to necessitate his hanging on a coatrack. Jeff was too big and mostly reclusive and no one since seventh grade had taken it upon themselves to single him out for degradation. He was the silent, nonmember of the class, and only the occasional studied insertion of meaningless but ambiguously obvious symbolism into his drawings gave him a character: Jeff was inscrutably deep, a true artist.

This story hinges on the substitution of conceptualization

for experience. This is not the lot of every gay teenager, though it does tend to produce adults who in their turn provide the concepts for the next generation. Jeff was a Reader; had learned how to understand his sexuality in terms of isolation, of misunderstanding, and by analogy, thought of himself as an artist. If I were to describe Jeff as painfully self-aware, that would imply a state of being, a quality of his person, and that is not what I mean to describe; self-awareness, in this case, is a mode of thinking, not an objective quality, a bad habit of reflecting on all possible choices of action and asking the metaphysical question "What does this mean?" as if one can supply the answer. As such, it reflects self-consciousness, which, at its root, springs from embarrassment.

Jeff was silently amazed by his deskmate Steve. He was a geek. This was plain to see, and not just as a cruel taunt from the preppy girls or redneck boys. Underweight, clownish looking in baggy clothes with the bright Memphis patterns of the early mid-eighties, with a round, pimply face and bulbous little nose. Irritatingly persistent sense of humor. But Steve was not aware that he was a geek. In fact, Jeff discovered, he regarded himself as a founding figure and leader of Cowtown's alternative scene. Jeff didn't quite know what exactly an alternative scene was, but gathered it had something to do with wearing big boots, stealing your father's big gray overcoat, and buying records, which was something Jeff hadn't discovered yet.

["And God help us all when I finally did!"]

And while Steve was this scene's princeling, his best friend, Trey, who occasionally wandered into the class and sat down, receiving only a scornful raised eyebrow from Freedman, was its undisputed king.

Trey wore earrings in both ears. His blond hair was long on the crown of his egg-shaped head and shaved on the sides. He wore a leather jacket and black boots. Jeff's homeroom was filled with sociable preppy boys whose executive fathers had moved them from near Baltimore to one of the superficially stately executive developments that had, in Jeff's short lifetime, come to dominate these northern farmlands, and these boys kindly informed Jeff that Trey Baloux was, simply, a big fag.

"You wanna go out with me tonight?' Steve asked Jeff as he stood in front of his open locker, his classmates wondering why on earth any senior'd be talking to him, even a geeky, outcast senior. Punks hung out in downtown Towson, the county seat, in the parking lot of the Burger King. There was no larger scene to hook up with, no downtown teenage friends with garage bands for them to copy. Jeff couldn't even skateboard so he was left out of that aspect.

Jeff sat on the trunk of Steve's Toyota, the minimal lights of Towson illuminating the unauthorized night life of Burger King's back lot, and soaked up stories of building skateboard ramps. "Man, my dad pulled down that quarter-pipe Mike 'n' I'd spent all last summer building," Brent, a wiry boy who looked just like the pictures of California skaters in magazines, was saying. At about ten-thirty, a murmur spread among the thirty or so boys and scattered punk girls. Almost spontaneously, or at least without a conscious understanding of the chain of cause and effect, the crowd leaders systematically instituted a massive roundup of boards and sticks that Jeff reluctantly took part in, for the impending rumble.

["like the Mods and the Rockers on Brighton Beach"]

—between themselves and the heavy-metal kids in their muscle cars.

"Here, take this." Steve handed Jeff a two-by-four with two rusty nails on the end, and he ended up cradling it in his arms all night, too nervous to throw it away, but praying to God that nothing would happen, that the red Nova would never come back down Allegheny Avenue. A white Volkswagen Rabbit, plastered with bumper stickers of the Jodie Foster's Army and Bones variety as well as orange and black spray paint, sped into the parking lot, squealing to a stop. Two boys jumped out, nervous with excitement and enthusiasm; one was Steve's friend Matt, a jovial, perpetually stoned Mormon with a wave of oily black hair that hung in his face. He'd ridden Jeff's school bus to elementary school, carrying a grotesquely large brown trombone case, and looked the same now as then, except his prodigious baby fat had turned into a round-faced cuteness. The other boy was tall, thin, clad in torn-up knee-length khakis with tall combat boots, torso unnaturally bulky with a black leather jacket. He twisted his head about as if smelling the air and a pouf of strawberry-blond trailed in slow motion, settling back over one side of his head. His head was too big for his neck.

"Trey!" Steve yelled, dropping the shortish pipe that would

have been no use in fighting anyhow. "C'mon, man. Those guys in the red Nova are fucking with us again."

"Man," he said, puckering his lower lip and blowing away the slightly starched wisp of hair that floated near his face. "They're not going to fight us." He leaned his butt back against the closed car door. "They're just driving around, looking for something to do. There's nothing to do." Then, without moving his gaze, which was directed toward Steve, he noticed Jeff off to one side. "Hey, Mr. Artist." Trey acknowledged him with a slight tilt of his chin.

Trey owned the only black leather jacket in Jeff's high school. He'd had it for a couple years, or else had bought it used—maybe more likely, considering how new this fashion was to Cowtown—and the gray lining hung inside it like tattered fur. Whenever Trey left it hanging on the back of a chair or on a table in the art room, Jeff would slip it on as if he were imitating Trey, as if he were mocking him really, sure of Trey's ultimately farcical essentiality. Meanwhile, he inhaled the entirely memorable odor the jacket contained, impressed enough to suppose that the ripe, complicated smell was a combination of Trey's armpits and moldy leather.

["It was Drakkar Noir, actually." There's an almost wistful look in Jeff's eyes. "Plus a minute personal variable, of course."]

And it was about this time when Jeff, left alone in his isolated clapboard house, tried on torn fishnets, black makeshift skirts he'd shortened himself, and dramatic red and black makeup. He imagined that in this outfit he could slip into a dimly lit downtown club and pass as a punkette. He might have been able to, actually, if he'd thought of a way to get there.

Jeff's mind felt pretty blank as he began his weekly sketch-book assignment, alone in the art room during C lunch. Standing by the blackboard, he placed the open eighteen-by-twenty-four sketchpad on the chalk ledge. Jeff traced the contours of an oblong head, the divisive angle of a line of hair falling across the face. He rapidly filled in the body, got to the spindly legs, disappearing into exaggeratedly huge boot tops. Jeff drew over the skeleton with red and black Magic Markers; the caricature of Trey emerged from the page. A black-edged bubble emerging from his mouth. "It's like, Hardcore . . . like, you know, Anarchy . . . like Punk Rock . . . You know, Hardcore."

"Does that look like Trey?" Jeff wondered with an acceptably passable ignorance in critique the next day. "I wasn't thinking about him." In subsequent drawings, Jeff reduced Trey's visage to a reproducible formula.

An exaggerated oblong formed his head proper.

Two lines, set close together, were his neck.

Two big dots, eyes; two littler dots, nostrils.

Tiny horizontal line, a mouth.

Squiggle at the top, that piece of hair that fell along his forehead.

A half-circle, T-shirt neck.

Two large shark fins, a diamond. Tiny triangles on the shoulder, Trey's jacket.

A lightning-bolt-and-skull earring dangling from the left ear.

This formula without fail creates an unmistakable and obvious portrait of Trey Baloux. Jeff improvised a form of print-making from mimeograph sheets and a clay burnisher, did a

Trey Baloux, rubbed it out forty times on a sheet of watercolor paper. The first sheet Jeff colored au natural, pink for the skin, orangy for the hair, blue-black for the jacket. The next sheet he tried random colorization. Sometimes Trey's skin would be blue, green, pink, the jacket yellow, red, black. He did it on colored sheets of paper. He made six-inch-high versions of the Trey stamps and filled a sheet of hundred-percent rag gray charcoal paper with eight big Treys. "That's me," Trey would say, in admiration of the reproduction of his image, his pride drowning out any potential apprehension over why Jeff might be creating this series.

"Why are you fascinated with him? Do you want to be him? What's the deal?" Mr. Freedman stood, hands on his hips of his round body. "All I know is I'm sick to death of seeing Trey Baloux's bony face."

"Don't know why you like him," Kristen muttered. "He's such a fag."

"Hey. Hey!" Freedman gave her chair a hard rap as he waddled by.

"Wanna go down to Club Unknown with us tonight?" Trey asked as Jeff sprawled out on his huge amorphous bed, an ordinary double mattress on milk crates plus the wandering forms of sheets, quilt, pillows, underwear, and loose cassettes. Club Unknown was in the basement of a community college's student center, and cost three dollars to get in. "A guy I know is deejaying tonight and's gonna play cool shit."

"Okay," Jeff said. An alternative to reading *The Red Pony* for English class on Monday. Trey threw his T-shirt on the bed near Jeff's ankles, and stood motionless for a moment, his pointy red nipples like buttons on his pale and well-ribbed chest. When he dropped his pants Jeff looked at him sort of, to show that he wasn't concerned with Trey's impending nakedness, but he also looked at other potential objects of interest; his Clash albums, his BMX bike posters. Jeff positioned the angle of his head so that Trey's pelvis area was at the periphery of his vision, and without evidently moving his eyes, got a good look at Trey's cock, fringed by a sparse ring of orangish hair, as he slipped out of his boxer shorts and hung them on the arm of his chair. Jeff got hard against the mattress as Trey stooped to pick up an undoubtedly smelly bath towel off the floor. He sat on the bed next to Jeff for a moment while he picked up and looked at tapes, before making his choice and inserting it in the stereo. In the blank before the music, he turned the volume hard to the right and strolled into the bathroom.

Underneath the wailings of Nina Hagen, Jeff listened to the shower pelt Trey's body, or splash loudly when he moved in the stall. He could smell moldy traces of crotch and lint in the grayed underwear scattered around him. Slowly he rubbed himself against the mattress, just a little. When he heard the water stop, he pulled his cock straight up and put the head under the waistband of his shorts so it wouldn't stick out. He pretended to ignore the reverse strip act, until Trey had a pair of black jeans thoroughly on and was starting on his socks. He smelled like cheap green stick deodorant and the hair under his arms was plastered into shiny wet spikes. He combed his hair straight back so that the rough edges of the long parts stuck out like a ledge over the darker stubble of the shaved back portion of his head.

"Cowtown didn't have a wealth of opportunities." Jeff is getting dressed to run to the store—*"tea bags and ciggie butts."* He thrusts his feet into stiff leather boots that come up a little over the ankles, and he wears these with red and white socks. Jeff has his hair loose now, and it hangs just to his shoulders, one length, chestnut-brown, like the hair his grandfather claims to have had before it fell out because of the Vaseline he used to slick it straight. "Trey wasn't actually gay, of course. Even though people said he was a fag and all. He actually got laid quite a bit. More than most of the jock guys. I don't think he had a clue why I liked him. And he never was very personal in his friendship with me."

"And that's a lucky thing," says George, "you sicko." And aside: "Imagine what he would have done if he'd actually found someone to go along with his literary fantasies."

Trey's Volkswagen was packed: him, Deedee, and Brent in the front seats; Jeff, Steve, and Mary and her brother Willie, whom Jeff had met a couple times, Mary being an Unknown regular, in the back. Jeff's legs were pressed up against the back of Deedee's seat, his scuffed red kneecaps sticking out through the dark blue plaid of his pants. Trey was bitching at the back-seaters for attempting to smoke and use the ashtray, which was located on the stick-shift island between the front seats. Willie had his head lying on the top of the seat, looking up, upside down from the rear window, watching the buildings of Charles Street grow progressively taller from that vantage.

"For Christ's sake, Rats, you can relax," Willie said, sitting up finally. Rats was the nickname he'd come up with, after the worn-out fox stole Jeff'd bought in Georgetown because it matched his fake hair color. "You don't have to sit all squished up like that." He roughly grasped Jeff's leg right above the knee, pulled it from its locked position. "That's better?" He nodded, an elfin leer from his nearly bald head with its fringe of blond Mohawk. Jeff nodded back with an idiot smile, and looked out the window.

Trey parked the car in the back lot of a business, in what looked to Jeff to be a seedier area of Baltimore, though only because he'd never before seen it at night. The lot next to this one featured a loudspeaker which blared, in a masculine computer voice, "This is private property. . . . Do not park your vehicle here . . . It will be towed away . . . This is private prop . . ."

"Lock your doors," Trey insisted, and marched haughtily down the alley to Maryland Avenue. Jeff was briefly shocked; he saw no nightclub, only closed-up storefronts, and a trio of shadowy homeless men congregating on the far street corner.

"Have you been here before?" Jeff asked no one in particular, but it turned out he was asking Mary, who was closest. Brent and Deedee held hands and rowdily bounced back and forth between the storefronts and the curb, and Steve and Willie produced the wailings of play-fights about a block back. Trey had walked directly to a painted aluminum warehouse door, and was knocking on it.

"Yeah," said Mary, as the door opened, setting free dance music and slivers of red light on the sidewalk. "It's pretty fun."

Jeff had been to underage night at Maxwell's, a suburban singles bar, and felt oppressed by the high school jocks who felt compelled to point out that Jeff's socks didn't match, as if they were still in their territory and outcast teenagers should respond appropriately to their presence. Jeff stared his nasty stare at them; didn't they realize? Here we were the boss, the cool kids. Trey dancing in between two girls grinding their miniskirted pelvises against his bony butt. Bottle-blond Deedee fighting off an assortment of beautiful skater boys, the same Deedee who had fake bloody maxi pads stuck to her locker door with notes that read, "fucking ugly bitch." And Jeff, sitting on top of a four-foot-high speaker in black shorts, army boots, black turtleneck, and red and gold bathrobe, flicking the butts of his Dunhill cigarettes onto the dance floor, acting as world-weary as he could manage with freshly dyed auburn hair hanging at the ordained length—covering the eyes. Trey got into a couple fights at Maxwell's, just wimpy touch-tag games in the parking lot, basically, and Maxwell's was cut off the list. But the Cygnet was legendary, a name with an aura of forbidden stuff.

["It was," says Jeff, "a cheesy gay juice bar that opened up once a week to underage kids."]

Deedee and Steve dropped its name regularly, and Jeff never right out said he'd never been there.

Jeff stepped into the entrance cubicle of Cygnet as Trey argued with the doorman; apparently there was one too many people for his guest allowance. So they crowded around the little desk the man was sitting at.

["An obviously gay man, pushing thirty and probably not too thrilled about the new kind of clientele."]

and Willie slipped behind them, onto the dance floor. The walls of the place were flat black, inscrutably dark, and the carpeting was bright red and black in an immense diamond pattern. Willie waved at Jeff from the edge of the dance pit. The doorman counted them again, got confused, let them go in, and the layout became apparent. Astonishing. A wooden dance floor was set down like a mini roller rink, around which ran a carpeted platform with spotlighted precipices on which the especially vain could dance.

"And that's where Trey went straightaway." Jeff laughs in recollection. "He had this peculiar dance he always did where he bent his knees, stuck out his rear end behind him, and jogged his arms and shoulders like a clock from the four o'clock to eight o'clock positions, bouncing his head in rhythm to the music." On his feet, Jeff demonstrates, quite naturally. "It was the first dance I'd ever learned. I wasn't very light on my feet, I was used to doing the little 'stick your feet out in rhythm, bounce slightly, don't move your arms or butt,' what my friend Kirsten called 'the straight boy dance.' Don't know why I went out dancing back then, 'cause I didn't like to; the next summer, when I went on a program to Paris, me and my friends slipped out to go to La Piscine (a club which was supposed to be extremely hip at the time, like the Palladium in New York or something—it was an old bathhouse, hence the name), and when I danced, I imitated Trey. But nobody knew that's what I was doing." Jeff shrugs. "And that's how I began to dance, a year later, on a different continent."

Willie elevated himself onto a black metal grid that towered over the floor, and pumped up and down on it, as if seeking to leap off but unaccountably restrained to this roost. Someone else thought he looked threateningly like he'd jump onto the dancers below, one of the bouncers unfortunately. Willie was a bit much for that place, his approximation of an angry young man too believable. His scrawny legs hung in midair for a second, tangled in the sleeves of the plaid shirt tied around his hips, and he decided not to—kick the bouncer? climb up higher? Whatever was in Willie's head, he simply jumped down onto the platform into the hostile embrace of the bouncer, with whom he walked into the darkness of the bar.

Jeff was not having fun. There was nobody to talk to.

["This was the attitude that got me, and still gets me, labeled a killjoy."]

Jeff was wearing ripped-up blue plaid pants, part of a suit of his father's circa 1978, a black tank top, his sprout of dyed red curls not in the least dampened by sweat. "Willie must be bored," Jeff figured, "so I'll go hang out with him."

"Hey, Rats," he said as Jeff cautiously peeked out the club door, not wanting to be kept out if he didn't see Willie. He was settled down on the stoop of a hardware store a few yards away.

"They throw you out?" Jeff asked.

"They don't like me there." He took the last drag of his cigarette, a Pall Mall. "I slammed there once and I guess it was really uncool. They're pretty uptight and all, 'cause of all the old people." Most of the club's clientele was late twenties, hip urban professional.

Jeff sat down next to him in the low lights of the street lamps.

"Is Trey still dancing in there?" He folded up his knees, placed his white-haired arms on top of them, his chin on top of that.

"Yeah." Jeff pulled out a red and gold pack of cigarettes, pulled one out and noticed the gesture of his mouth, open, tongue slightly protruding, eyes fixed on Jeff's hand. Jeff gingerly placed the filter end on the exposed pink lining of his bottom lip. His mouth shut on it like a trap. Jeff removed a second cigarette for himself, and lit them with his father's silver Zippo.

"Thanks." Willie laughed, taking the first drag. "Yeah. Trey likes to dance." He untied the shirt from around his waist, draped it over his shoulders, like an old woman. His Mohawk, nine inches of fine yellow hair, lay on Jeff's side of his face, silk over stubble, with the shell-like edge of his ear poking through. "How'd you meet Trey?" He blew smoke effortlessly in dual plumes from his nose.

"We go to school together."

"Cowtown?" He snorted, then coughed, his frame vibrating. "Man, that place's beat." Willie's from Lutherville, more suburban, infinitesimally less beat. "Yeah, Trey and Steve've talked about you. You ought to come out with us more."

"Remember when we went to Georgetown during Energy Week, last February?"

"That was you?" He scrunched up his nose. "Yeah, I guess that was you. Looked pretty normal then though."

"I've never been particularly normal."

"Well, join the club. I know the difference between looking and being."

Jeff let his shoulders slump, just a little.

"This time last year," Willie told him, "I looked pretty straight myself."

"Straight?"

"You know. Uptight, normal." He cocked his head. "What'd'ja think I meant?" Jeff sat uncomfortably in his scuffed penny loafers, his rear end cold against the cement. "Did you think I meant like, straight versus gay?"

"No," said Jeff, with finality.

"I don't think I look very gay." Jeff looked at Willie quizzically. Willie laughed. Jeff didn't.

Willie stopped laughing, the kind of cutoff you give a laugh when you realize you're telling a joke about death to someone whose mother just died, or, maybe, when you're telling a joke with a dirty punch line to someone's parents that you thought were hip, but whose faces are turning sourer the further along you get. "And I'm not," Willie said, in nervous humor, "very gay."

"I'm not very gay either," Jeff added in seriousness. Willie wore a severe, melancholy expression, then laughed outright, retreated back into moribundity, only to break into an irrepressible smile again.

"The young homosexual is especially adept at recognizing others like himself," Willie repeated.

"What?" Jeff asked, bewildered, before sensing the presence of irony.

["And Americans can't tell the difference between irony and sarcasm anyhow," says George.]

"Oh, yeah." Willie scrutinized Jeff's expression. "You're scared shitless, aren't you?"

"Do you have a boyfriend?"

"No." His hand rubbing the stubble of his head. "Where do you get boyfriends in Baltimore?"

"Have you ever kissed a boy?"

"If I'd kissed a boy"—Willie's face was toward the sky—"I'd probably consider him my boyfriend."

"Do you think Trey's gay?" Jeff asked him, idly rubbing his chin with his hand.

"Oh, please." Willie turned his head, his warm and slightly rank breath in Jeff's face. "Trey fucks more girls than you or I'd know what to do with. Trey is such a straight boy." Jeff looked dead ahead, into the black roadway, glistening with glass fragments. He rubbed his hands along his bare upper arms. "You cold?" Grabbing the sleeve of his flannel shirt, he balled it up in his lap. Taking it by the shoulders, he laid it across Jeff's back, patting it on. He left his hand there.

"Willie, I want to go back in."

"You want to go back in the club?" Jeff nodded. "You do like me, kinda?"

"I don't want to sit on the street."

Letting the weight of his feet ballast him upward, Willie stood erect and extended his hand down to Jeff. He stood up, the top of Willie's head came just to his chin. The stripe of blond hair formed a perfect line down the center of his skull. They walked the half block to Cygnet's door. Willie dropped Jeff's hand, which Jeff hardly noticed he'd been holding. It felt moist, then cold in the free air. "You'll see me again, okay?" Willie said.

Inside the club, Trey was dancing with an older black woman who was probably an office worker by day; tonight, she was a svelte creature of the night, shimmying with a nineteen-year-old white boy, and she'd turn and smile at her two friends, dancing more decorously with men their own age. Deedee and Mary were drinking red punch, spiked out of a little bottle Mary'd had in her purse. Brent and Steve chatted up some awfully well-made-up thirteen-year-olds, compatible in size, though Deedee threw Brent disapproving looks when she thought about it. Willie tugged on Mary's arm. "Sis, you wanna go home?" Deedee shook her head, no. "Man, we can take a cab home, it's not so far."

"Stop, Willie, we're going soon." Deedee leapt off the barstool and found Trey in the crowd. "It's all right," she said, returning. "Trey's found some friends here, he said we can take the car and go home."

Deedee dropped Mary and Willie in front of a gray house in a Lutherville neighborhood; Mary jumped off Jeff's lap, kissed me on the cheek, waved. "Call me, Deedee," she said mechanically.

"Dudes." Willie crawled over the backseat, scrambling to his feet. "See you." He held out his hand to me, doing some funny handshake that Jeff couldn't follow. "Rats." He nodded, then smiled. The light at the door went on as Mary searched for her keys. "Later."

George purses his lips, looks dubious.

"Of course," says Jeff, answering that look, "this is a compilation of a lot of things that had an influence on my life at the time."

"No kidding," George says deadpan.

"Physically, the skinniness, the 'elfin leer,' the blond Mohawk, is Billy Schwartz, whose father owned a Cadillac dealership, and I only met him once, on a day trip we all took to Georgetown. I remember watching him run along the creosoted railroad ties at the edge of the canal, throwing empty beer bottles he'd found in the parking lot upward toward planes taking off at the airport across the Potomac. He definitely wasn't gay."

"Sitting outside the club, that was this boy named Jimmy, who was an engineering student at Johns Hopkins when Trey was at art school. Trey would have these parties at his apartment where he'd set up two turntables and deejay hardcore singles all night long, and everyone he'd invited would sit around talking to each other, brought together only by the fact that Trey knew each of us. Jimmy was older, but one night he sat down with me and my friend Kirsten and we sang songs together; later that night, after the buses stopped running, he gave Kir and I a ride back into the country. A couple weeks later, Jimmy showed up at one of these parties with his girlfriend Dana, they'd just been to see *Cats* together. When they left, I told them I'd like to sleep with them sometime. It went over like a pretty witty thing to say, which I guess is more or less what I intended.

"And the thing with the leg in the car, that was Trey's room-mate John, one of three guys he lived with. They were friends at the beginning of the school year, and he'd go out with us sometimes, but he told Trey he was gay, and after that, Trey didn't like to hang out with him anymore. I never said a word about it."

While Jeff's out at the store, George begins filling us in on some of the less savored moments of Jeff's life. "Last year, Jeff ran away from New York City after his first boyfriend broke up with him. Did the Holden Caulfield thing and took a room in the Belvedere Hotel where he stayed for three days before he called me and had me come get him. He made a pass at me that weekend, in terms so polite and noncommittal I had to laugh at it. He knew he was being silly before he'd even asked. 'Would it be all right if I gave you a blow job?' is how he worded it, and there was a terror in his eyes as if this was the most important thing he'd ever asked of someone."

He scratches his elbow, glances towards the brass alarm clock sitting on the floor near the wall. "I had to tell him that I proba-bly couldn't get it up for him. 'You're just too ugly.' " He makes a facial expression, the equivalent to a shrug. "He accepted that line of reasoning. Not that Jeff's really that ugly or anything."

The door scratches loudly as it swings open over the warped linoleum. "What are you saying about me?" Jeff yells from the kitchen.

"Nothing," George says, "I'm telling 'em about the time you wanted to suck my dick."

"Oh, fuck you," Jeff says, offhand.

———

"Gallant," Trey began, "excuses himself into the bathroom when he has to fart."

Jeff gazed out the car window, reflecting on the two cartoon boys, how they'd react in the same situation. "Goofus says to his dinner guests, 'Hey, pull my finger.' " Jeff subtly adjusted his shorts underneath the black satin dress he was wearing; they were on their way to Deedee's Halloween party. "Gallant returns his sister's underwear neatly pressed to her top drawer after he's jerked off smelling them."

"Well . . ." Trey strove vainly for something even more disgusting. "Goofus jerks off on his sister's panties and keeps them to suck on."

"Well, how can I top that?" Jeff mused. The hair on his thighs felt springy under the weight of the fabric. He hadn't worn pantyhose. That seemed too much of a commitment.

"Who all's going to be at this party anyhow?"

"I dunno. Deedee's already over there, I guess Steve and Matt and Brent; Mary, Kirsten. Maybe Billy Schwartz, maybe Jimmy. Some people from Dulaney High." He stole a glance at Jeff's folded hands, glittering with silver and onyx skull rings Jeff had borrowed from him. "You sure you'll feel all right dressed like that?"

"Is that boy Willie going to be there?"

"I don't know, man, Willie's kind of a drag." Trey kept his eyes on the road. "I don't really like Willie." He switched on the wipes as plops of water began falling on the windshield. "Willie's a fag, I think."

The top of the dress, Jeff's sister's, felt tight against his chest. "Why do you think that?"

"Something Mary told Deedee."

Jeff visualized Trey Baloux, walking defiantly through the halls of Cowtown Junior-Senior, impervious to the murmurings which surrounded him like a royal fanfare. "What d'you mean, he's a fag?"

"What's wrong with you? What do you think it means?" He gripped the steering wheel tightly, his knuckles turning white, the black rubber and silver bangles around his bony wrists bouncing with the car's motion.

Jeff lit up a cigarette, winded down the window. Trey didn't like smoking in his car, and Jeff was mad at him. "I can't believe you threw him over because of bullshit like that."

"Man . . ." He shook his head. "You just don't understand."

A song Jeff liked came on WHFS, the Velvet Underground, "Sunday Morning."

"Deedee asked me if I was sleeping with him." The tone of his voice had softened.

"Trey, I don't really care, okay?" Jeff flicked the butt end out the window, watched it spark against the backseat window behind him. A few light drops of rain blew inside, but the air felt cool. "Sunday Morning" ended; the Smiths came on the radio, their new single, "The Boy with the Thorn in His Side."

"It's not any of your business to complain about. He wasn't your friend."

Jeff couldn't remember the number of the house we'd dropped Willie off at, nor the street. Jeff didn't even know his last name.

"Still they don't believe us," Morrissey lamented.

The radio turned off with a snap of Trey's wrist. "I was listening to that, thank you."

"I hate the fucking Smiths, man." Was Trey sulking? It'll be worse with no music, Jeff thought, and only the sound of rain on the hood. Jeff truly wished he was home watching *Mr. Belvedere* or something, rather than heading out for the night with a guy who, at this moment, he hated.

"Are you sleeping with him?" Jeff managed an accusing tone.

Trey flinched. "What the fuck is this?" He slammed his open palm against the steering wheel. "Why don't you and Deedee get together and talk about what a fag I am? Okay?" He pulled the car over to the side of the road, the wheels bouncing over the crumbling asphalt. "Get the fuck out of my car." He reached across Jeff's thighs to the handle, popping open the door.

"What are you waiting for?" Trey demanded, looking straight ahead.

"Trey, I was just asking 'cause . . ."

"I stick up for you, man." The muscles of his jaw vibrated. "They say the same shit about you and I stick up for you." He crossed his arms. "You can walk home from here."

Jeff stepped out of the car into the heavy rain. His shoes sank into the mass of decomposing leaves. Trey placed his hand on the gearshift, and sat still. The dyed curls of his hair soon hung limply in front of Jeff's eyes, water spiraling off the tips. The dress clung to his body, his boxer shorts showing through.

Trey leaned over, pushed the door open. "Get in." Jeff sat down, the wet vinyl sticking to his ass. Trey shook his head, shifted into forward, and turned the car around in the middle of the road. "I forgot you're wearing that stupid dress."

"How much of that story is a lie?" George asks.

"All of it," Jeff says. "Stories are. Fiction is a pack of lies."

About the Author

C. BARD COLE is the author of *Tattooed Love Boys* and six other illustrated chapbooks, and the co-creator of the zine *Riotboy*. Originally from Baltimore County, Maryland, he attended Sarah Lawrence College and Parsons School of Design. He lives in Manhattan's East Village, where he works as a graphic designer and organizes the fiction reading series Readings A Go Go.